A STORMY SEASON

Imperilled Young Widows, Book 4

Melanie Dickerson

GraceFaith Press

ASIN : B0BGYQG5D6

ISBN-13: 9798849485560

Cover design by: Erin Dameron-Hill

Printed in the United States of America

To Aaron
I have found the one
my soul loves

CONTENTS

BOOKS BY MELANIE DICKERSON

IMPERILED YOUNG WIDOWS SERIES
A Perilous Plan
A Treacherous Treasure
A Deadly Secret
A Stormy Season

REGENCY SPIES OF LONDON SERIES
A Spy's Devotion
A Viscount's Proposal
A Dangerous Engagement

THE DERICOTT TALES
Court of Swans
Castle of Refuge
Veil of Winter
Fortress of Snow
Cloak of Scarlet

A MEDIEVAL FAIRY TALE SERIES
The Huntress of Thornbeck Forest
The Beautiful Pretender
The Noble Servant

FAIRY TALE ROMANCE SERIES
The Healer's Apprentice
The Merchant's Daughter
The Fairest Beauty
The Captive Maiden
The Princess Spy
The Golden Braid
The Silent Songbird
The Orphan's Wish
The Warrior Maiden
The Piper's Pursuit
The Peasant's Dream

SOUTHERN SEASONS SERIES
Magnolia Summer

Chapter One

Jane Gilchrist glanced around the ballroom. The social season had hardly begun, as it was not yet Easter, so only half the usual guests filled the ballroom. And it seemed all the ladies present were at one end of the room, crowded around one man—Mr. Luke Watley, the young widower from Hertfordshire.

Jane forced herself not to roll her eyes to the ceiling. Why were young ladies who were clever in all the ways of Society, whose manners were otherwise impeccable, who had learned to speak other languages and play the pianoforte with great skill, so willing to make fools of themselves for the sake of one eligible young man in their midst?

Luke Watley was handsome; she could give him that. And he was young and rich. Those were all desirable traits in a husband, and many ladies were willing to give up the first two qualities if the gentleman was very rich. So perhaps she could understand them vying for the attentions of a man who possessed all three. But since that man had chosen so poorly in marrying his first wife, Anne Bailey, and as that first wife had passed away only three months ago, Jane was bothered by the fact that the ladies were making a spectacle at the expense of their own dignity.

"Just look at them," Lady Ingraham said, whispering as she came to stand beside Jane. "So eager to catch themselves a handsome widower." Lady Ingraham —Sarah, as Jane knew her—gave a snide smile in the direction of the ladies who were practically begging for Mr. Watley's attention.

A little pang assailed Jane as she remembered her brother Henry scolding her for being judgmental of others. Did she ever sound as cruel as Sarah did just now?

"I'm glad you have more dignity than that," Sarah went on. "You would never behave in such a way. In fact, I have heard you say that you'd rather be a spinster ten times over than throw yourself at a man the way young ladies are so wont to do these days."

Sarah's amusement at those ladies' expense made Jane rethink her own silent criticism. And Sarah could hardly disparage anyone, in Jane's opinion, since she'd married a man old enough to be her own grandfather.

Jane didn't want to be ridiculed and held in contempt for running after a marriageable gentleman, but . . . she did want to get married. She didn't want to just watch everyone else her age becoming mistress of a home and having children. She loved her brother Henry and her sister-in-law Penelope, but sometimes it was difficult to watch them staring adoringly into each other's eyes, giving each other those secret smiles, year after year, while she was still unmarried.

She didn't want to be lonely.

But she also couldn't bear to marry the wrong person, and being married didn't necessarily mean she wouldn't be lonely. Penelope had once described her first marriage as the loneliest years of her life. What if Jane made a similar mistake? What if she married someone who ignored her, was unfaithful, or was angry all the time? She could not bear it. And there was no recourse for a woman, or a man, usually, whose spouse turned out to be intolerable.

Jane wanted to marry for love, but she had to be wise about who she fell in love with.

What if she married someone about whose character she was badly mistaken, as Mr. Luke Watley had done?

Mr. Watley had married a woman of loose morality. Everyone whispered about Mrs. Watley, as she would leave her husband and child at their country home in Hertfordshire and go to London to attend parties and balls. She flirted shamelessly with every gentleman who gave her his attention, and it was rumored that she was the paramour of more than one man, including a Member of Parliament and a Frenchman of questionable reputation.

And then, three months ago, Mrs. Watley had been run over by a carriage in the middle of the street.

It was a tragic accident, but Jane had heard more than one person say it was poetic justice and "a mercy for her poor husband and child."

Such talk had seemed cold and cruel to Jane, but the unfortunate truth of the statements was only too clear.

Her brother Henry had known Mr. Watley since they were children. He said the man had been shattered by the news of his wife's sudden and violent death.

Henry had visited and consoled with him, telling Penelope and Jane afterward, "Luke is genuinely grieving his wife's death, but I believe some of his grief may be from having to face the reality of her character, having discovered that she was unfaithful."

"Why would a woman be unfaithful to a good man like Mr. Watley?" Penelope had asked in a hushed, horrified voice. "I cannot understand." Penelope was so kind and good, she was obviously at a loss.

"I suppose it was her uncertain upbringing, as she was an orphan brought up by an uncle of scandalous reputation," Henry said, shaking his head. "I tried to give Watley a hint before he married her that there were rumors of her character, but he would have none of it, saying it was all false gossip. And he married her so quickly, he didn't have time to see her true nature, I suppose."

"Well, I daresay he shall have enough young ladies vying for him now that he's a widower. He shall be happily remarried soon," Jane had said.

"That's a bit callous, don't you think?" Henry said.

How she hated when he scolded her, especially when he was right.

Her words seemed to be coming true, however, as she and Sarah watched the ladies smiling and laughing, the bolder ones even lightly touching his arm with a fan or gloved hand. But as she watched them, she noticed that Mr. Watley never smiled back at them. He was polite, nodding or speaking to them as was appropriate, but he did not flirt.

He looked somehow different from the way he'd looked before Mrs. Watley had died.

Before he met his wife, Jane had thought him a good marriage prospect for herself, if she was honest. He was serious and did not drink too much, and Henry said he did not sit at the gaming tables wasting his money or keep company with wastrels and those of bad character. "He is a good sort of fellow," Henry had said more than once. He'd even invited him to their home, and Jane suspected Henry had hoped she and his friend would make a match.

As soon as Jane realized this, she'd carefully avoided showing any interest in Mr. Watley.

Had that been foolish? She now wondered. She was getting older and her pool of prospects seemed to grow smaller every year.

But if the man was so foolish as to become entangled with, and even to marry, such a woman as Anne Bailey, then perhaps he was not a good match for Jane. She wanted to respect her husband, not feel sorry for him. And her determination remained strong to marry a gentleman who met all her requirements. She would not settle for less than her ideal, even if it meant she never married. Better to be alone than to lose her self-respect, married to a man of poor character or intelligence.

Long before the evening was over, Mr. Watley spoke to the hosts and apparently excused himself and departed early from the ball, for she did not see him again.

He may not have encouraged the young ladies' attentions to him, but it still did not sit well with Jane that he was so fawned over, especially since, unlike Sarah, Jane did not enjoy feeling contempt for her own kind.

Jane did not wish to be seen going out of her way to flirt with the newly widowed Luke Watley, but she sincerely hoped he would rally from his disappointments and choose more wisely next time he married.

~ ~ ~

Luke awakened so suddenly it took him a moment to realize he'd been dreaming.

His heart was pounding. *It was only a dream,* he repeated to himself, wishing he could erase the memory of it from his mind. But when he closed his eyes and lay back on his pillow, the image assaulted him afresh—his wife screaming as she was trampled by the horses and run over by the carriage wheels.

In the dream he'd tried to call out to her, to warn her that the runaway carriage was bearing down on her. But he was too late, and the whole thing happened slowly, as the horses first knocked her down, then . . . He'd woken himself up trying to shout her name.

He sat up again, this time throwing the covers off and getting out of bed. He'd go check in on Jeffrey.

He made his way to the nursery in the dark, keeping a hand on the wall, as there was only the barest bit of light coming in the windows from the moon outside. But the nursery was close—he had moved to the closest bedroom so he could be nearer where his son slept, and to escape as many memories as possible in his old room.

Luke opened the door and moved carefully, trying not to make any noise. A candle burning in a brass candlestick nearby illuminated his two-year-old son, lying on his back in the child-sized bed, and the nurse, Sally, asleep in another bed two feet away.

As Luke drew closer, Jeffrey's eyelids flickered, then stilled.

His face was so innocent and peaceful. The poor child did not understand that he no longer had a mother, that he would grow up without knowing the unconditional, unstoppable love of the person who had birthed him.

But he might not have known that love even if his mother had not died.

Luke covered his sleeping son with the blanket that his restless legs always kicked off sooner or later and left the room as quietly as possible, thanking God that Jeffrey had not been awakened; if he had seen Luke, it would have taken a long time to get him back to sleep.

Heading back to his bedroom, Luke went to the window that overlooked the stables. No one was stirring yet, as it was only about three in the morning according to the clock on the fireplace mantel. He wondered if he should light a lantern and go for a walk. He wanted to be sure that nightmare was completely off his mind before he went back to bed.

His thoughts drifted back to his son as he stared at the three-quarter moon. Jeffrey hardly ever mentioned his mother, as she had usually been away from him more than she was with him. Anne was forever thinking of any excuse to go to London and leave her son and husband at home in Hertfordshire. Luke had grown tired of trying to force her to stay with him. He didn't want to believe that she was actually being unfaithful to him, but in his heart he knew it was true. Too many people had seen too many suspicious things, and he had seen some of them himself.

A couple of his friends had insinuated that he should be thankful to God to be free of her. And perhaps he should. But Luke had gone to his uncle Edmund, the man he trusted most in the world, and told him, "Everyone wonders why I am mourning her, but I loved her. I was her protector, and she was my wife, the mother of my child. Everyone expects me to be cold and unfeeling about her now that she has died so suddenly, but how can

I? I find I am not equal to such a task."

Uncle Edmund had given him that serious, wise look of his and said, "You are not a fickle man. You are not so changeable or shallow as most others these days. It is no wonder your emotions cannot turn so quickly and irrevocably from love to hate. You must give yourself permission to grieve as long as you need to. But when your grieving is done, be wise enough to also allow an end to it."

These words made sense to Luke.

So far he had mourned Anne's death, but perhaps even more, he had mourned the loss of hope that she might be innocent of the much-gossiped-about unfaithfulness, the hope that she might learn to be happy and content to be his wife and Jeffrey's mother.

He'd also mourned the loss of his own reputation.

He was well aware that everyone saw him as a dupe, a cuckolded, foolish, humiliated husband of a woman who would betray him with more than one man.

Never in his life had he imagined he'd repeat his own father's mistake. His father had been so heartbroken by the death of Luke's mother when Luke was ten years old that he had immediately remarried—within two months, in fact—just to stop the pain. But the woman he'd married was so similar in nature and behavior to Anne that Luke had berated himself over and over for not seeing it.

It was humiliating enough to have a father who was so fooled in his wife's character, but much more humiliating to repeat the mistake himself. His father, who refused to believe what everyone was telling him about his faithless wife, had gone to his grave defending her. At least Luke now accepted the truth of what his wife had done.

He let out a long, uneasy breath, leaning against the window and rubbing his face with his hands.

Even though Luke had wondered how his father could have remarried so quickly, he had recently been tempted to do the same thing for the same reason— to stop the pain. But the thought of making the same mistake again filled him with such dread that the temptation was soon overcome.

How could he ever trust another woman again?

And in fact, he wondered if he could trust anyone. One of the men Anne was rumored to have been involved with was a Frenchman, Louis Lenoir, who Henry Gilchrist said was connected with a group of revolutionaries— a secret, seditious society bent on overthrowing the government. Henry was on a committee that was investigating them.

"The man could be dangerous," Henry told him after Anne's death, "so if you see him following you, send me word immediately."

"But he could have nothing to do with me, surely," Luke had said.

"Perhaps not, but . . . we have reason to believe that he may have had something to do with your wife's accident. Indeed, it may not have been an accident at all."

"Why do you say this?" Luke wasn't sure if his anger at Henry was justified, but surely he could trust his old friend. "Tell me what you know."

"Forgive me for being the one to tell you this," Henry said, "but the carriage that was involved in the accident belonged to Lenoir's associate, a Mr. Bassett. It could be a coincidence."

Luke's stomach churned and he was afraid he

might be sick.

Henry kindly remained silent for a few moments, allowing Luke to steel himself.

When Luke was able to speak calmly, he said, "I am willing to do as you ask, but I don't know what this Lenoir looks like. How will I recognize him?"

"I have a couple of sketches provided by our spies who have spent some time in his company." Henry produced two rolled-up parchment sketches, one a frontal view and the other a side view. Both showed a man with dark hair, a mustache, and a long, angular face.

So this was the man his wife had betrayed him for. Not only was he not handsome, but he looked to be twenty years older.

"Have you seen him before?" Henry asked.

"No."

"He is tall, about your height, and he is known to carry a pistol concealed inside his cloak. If you see him, even if you don't know if he is following you, send me word."

Luke nodded, heat rising up into his neck and forehead, contrasting with a coldness in his gut. What was this new feeling? Was it bitterness? The Holy Scriptures warned against allowing a root of bitterness to grow, but Luke found the bitterness preferable to the pain, embarrassment, and crushing sadness.

Perhaps it was time to stop mourning and start fighting.

"If there is anything I can do to help stop these revolutionaries, Henry, enlist me. I'm ready and willing to help."

"You will be known to this man. It would be neither safe nor effective for you to be involved with our investigation. I'm sorry."

Luke blew out a forceful breath.

"We'll get him, sooner or later," Henry had said, clapping him on the back. "In the meantime, take care of yourself and little Jeffrey."

Now, as Luke stared out the window as the first grayness of dawn approached, he realized he was getting better, feeling less desperate than he had for the first month after Anne's death. To be honest, he hardly remembered anything about those days, so dark were they.

He had to be strong for Jeffrey. As Luke himself was an orphan, he often reminded himself that he didn't want Jeffrey to be completely without family at the tender age of two. He had to live and overcome this painful trial, for Jeffrey's sake.

Chapter Two

Jane enjoyed springtime in London, though perhaps not as much as spring in the country. But her job as bookkeeper and half-owner of a clothing shop kept her in London. Besides, the overcrowded metropolis did possess some lovely parks, and Jane often walked around Hyde Park in the morning before anyone else was awake, her favorite time of day to be in nature.

Fog hung heavy in the air. Even fewer people were out than usual. An older man was taking his morning exercise. A young man was breaking in a new horse. Otherwise, Jane was alone as she enjoyed the moody appearance of the fog against the cloudy sky, the drops of moisture covering every tree and bush and blade of grass.

A child's playful laugh broke through her thoughts. Moments later a little boy jumped from behind a bush a few feet in front of her. He must have been about two or three years old. His bright blue eyes met Jane's and his smile sent a strange sensation straight to her heart.

The child's blond curls were nothing short of beautiful, but his mischievous grin, square chin, and wide forehead were distinctly boyish. He suddenly ran to her, took her hand, and ordered, "Come!"

Jane willingly went with him. "Where is your

nurse?" Surely he was not alone.

"There you are," a masculine voice said. Luke Watley stood before her, his gaze bouncing from the boy to Jane.

The child squealed, then laughed, obviously delighted with their game.

"Forgive me," Mr. Watley said. "I'm afraid my son has never been shy of strangers. Come, Jeffrey." He reached for the child's hand.

"No!" Jeffrey was still grinning, but he shrank away from his father and pressed into Jane, wrapping an arm around her leg through the layers of her cloak and dress.

"We must allow this lady to be on her way. Come." Mr. Watley looked up at Jane, raising his brows. "Please forgive us."

Jeffrey giggled as if it was a hilarious game they were playing.

"Nothing to forgive," Jane said, and squatted beside the boy, taking his hand in hers. "Are you playing hide-and-seek? May I play too?"

He nodded, then darted away. His father made a move to snatch him, but Jeffrey remained just out of reach, still giggling adorably.

"Please excuse me. I am so sorry," Mr. Watley called as he ran past.

Jane hid her laugh behind her hand as she watched the man chase his son down. He swung Jeffrey up in his arms and around in a circle, then tossed him in the air a few inches, catching him and sending the child into peals of laughter. Then he started back toward Jane, carrying Jeffrey under his arm as if he was a sack of flour.

"Forgive my bad manners. Miss Jane Gilchrist, is it?"

"Yes, and you are Mr. Luke Watley."

"I am, and this is my incorrigible son, Jeffrey."

Jeffrey was struggling to get away. "Down!" he cried.

"Tell Miss Gilchrist you are sorry for grabbing onto her, for that is not how a gentleman treats a lady." He set the child gently on the ground.

Jeffrey looked uncertainly at Jane. "I sorry." Immediately he grabbed her hand again and demanded, "You play."

Jane couldn't help laughing. "What shall we play?"

"Chase me!" he said, and started running.

On his short little legs Jeffrey was easy to catch, but Jane only pretended to run, saying, "You run so fast!" while trotting along behind him.

How thankful she was that no one was in the park to see her! They would surely think she was flirting with Mr. Watley, making herself ridiculous by playing with his son in the park, more shameless than those young ladies hovering around him two nights ago at the ball.

But she was not flirting with Mr. Watley. She enjoyed small children. They were adorable and innocent and unspoiled by the world. They didn't judge, weren't ashamed of anyone or anything, and were unfailingly honest. And Mr. Watley's motherless child was as adorable as any little boy she'd ever seen. How could she ever say no to a request to play with him?

Jane caught hold of the back of Jeffrey's clothes, then pretended she couldn't hold on and let go. This sent the child into more squeals and peals of laughter.

Finally, he stopped and fell to the ground, turning those big, beautiful eyes on her, almost begging to be tickled. So she obliged, gently tickling his sides. He laughed again, but then she stopped tickling him so he could catch his breath. He lay staring up at her with the most serene smile on his lips.

"I am afraid you have done it now," Mr. Watley whispered, while the child was chattering to himself. "He doesn't relinquish playmates easily. He will probably demand you come home with him and play for the rest of the day."

"Chase me," Jeffrey said, pushing up onto his feet and motioning to Jane.

She chased him until he got distracted by the young man nearby who was giving his horse different commands—galloping, then trotting, stopping and walking, then galloping again.

A few more people were now out taking their morning exercise, and most of them were watching Jane and Mr. Watley and his son scampering about the park. And Jane could just imagine what they were thinking and saying behind their gloved hands. No doubt they were accusing Jane of running after Mr. Watley while pretending interest in his child. But let them talk. Though Jane despised being misunderstood, not to mention being accused of throwing herself at a man, she mustn't let other people dictate how she spent her time.

She caught Mr. Watley glancing around at the people watching them, including a man who suddenly turned and walked away.

"We really should go." Mr. Watley's countenance was abruptly sober. He picked up his wriggling son. "Forgive us for taking up your time, Miss Gilchrist."

"Not at all. I enjoyed playing with Jeffrey."

Jane forced herself not to take Jeffrey's outstretched hand as the child began to call out, "Miss Gilch'ist!" mimicking his father, though unable to say the *r* in her name. But Mr. Watley was obviously determined to part from her, as he turned and walked away with his son still calling out and starting to cry.

Well, that was abrupt. Had Mr. Watley been so afraid of the gossips speaking ill of Jane that he would take his son and depart, as if his life depended on getting away from her? Or had he seen someone in particular who had compelled him to go? Either way, his behavior seemed odd.

She needn't care what Mr. Watley thought any more than she cared about the gossips. But her heart did ache a little at the last sight of the handsome boy still reaching out to her as he rounded a bend in the path, his high-pitched voice calling out to her.

~ ~ ~

Luke instantly recognized the man in the park as Louis Lenoir. The man who had been with Anne.

Luke managed to abstain from catching up to the man and punching him in the face—but only because he had Jeffrey with him. Jeffrey was more important. Even so, it was impossible not to imagine slamming his fist into the man's nose and mouth, over and over.

God, help me.

He hated to be so abrupt with Miss Jane Gilchrist, especially since she was Henry's sister, but he knew it would be difficult to convince Jeffrey that he couldn't take up all of the young woman's time. Luke had been on the brink of trying to politely and delicately extricate Jeffrey from this new playmate when he'd spotted that weaselly looking man staring at them.

Lenoir. He obviously knew who Luke was, as he hurried away as soon as he saw that Luke had recognized him.

Luke's blood boiled anew just thinking about the skulking man with his long black cloak.

He would challenge the man to a duel. But that was foolish, most importantly because Jeffrey needed his father. Besides that, if Luke was killed, he would look like a cuckolded man who was a bad shot. And though he did wish Lenoir dead, he didn't particularly wish to be the one to kill him. Such a thing would become common knowledge immediately and follow him for the rest of his life. No, *"Vengeance is mine. I will repay," saith the Lord.* Luke would not kill the man.

Unless of course he was provoked and forced to defend himself.

"Miss Gilchrist play wif me," Jeffry wailed, his tears and runny nose creating quite a mess on Luke's shoulder.

"Perhaps Miss Gilchrist will play with you again soon."

"Today?"

"Probably not, but your nurse Sally is happy to play with you. She's waiting for you at home, I daresay."

Jeffrey laid his head down, still whining softly, but when they were almost home, he started breathing deeply and evenly, indicating he had fallen asleep.

As Luke approached his townhouse, he saw that the front door was slightly ajar. The hair on the back of his neck prickled. Something felt wrong.

He pushed the door open. When he did, he heard shouting from one of the male servants and a woman's scream.

Highly aware of Jeffrey asleep on his shoulder, Luke mentally calculated how quickly he could grab the poker from the nearest fireplace as he stepped inside. He called out, "Who's there?"

A maidservant's indistinct voice came from the stairs that led from the entry hall down to the lower level. Luke proceeded toward it, glancing all around as he went.

He stopped, looked down from the top of the stairs, and saw the butler lying on the floor by the bottom step, dark red blood on his cheek and just above his eyebrow, running down his temple.

One of the housemaids was kneeling on the floor beside him. She cried out, "Sir! Someone has injured Cobb."

"Did anyone see who did this?" Luke went into the sitting room and grabbed the iron poker in his free hand. As he emerged, one of the footmen, Burke, met him in the hallway.

"Is the intruder still in the house?" Luke asked.

"I don't know, sir."

"Is Cobb badly hurt?"

"He's bleeding from the head and hasn't opened his eyes yet, but he still breathes. Smith has gone to fetch a surgeon."

"Are the rest of the servants accounted for? Where's Sally?"

"I am here, sir." Sally appeared behind him and followed him as he began climbing the staircase to his bedroom to fetch his gun. "Shall I take Jeffrey?"

"No, I've got him. I want to make certain the man who harmed Cobb is not still here."

"He hit him and shoved him down the stairs. We are all rather frightened," Sally said.

"Did anyone see the man?"

"I was at the bottom of the stairs, but I only caught a glimpse as he struck Cobb and made him fall. It was a horrible sight." Sally's voice was breathy and hushed.

"Then he ran toward the back of the house."

"What did you see of the man?"

"Only that he was taller than Cobb. His hat was pulled down low, and to be honest, sir, I didn't see his face."

When Luke reached the top of the stairs, he opened the first door on the right, which was his own bedroom. Clothing was strewn everywhere and furniture was overturned.

Luke went in cautiously and headed for the bedside table. He opened the drawer and cursed under his breath. His pistol was missing, just as he'd suspected.

Of course the intruder would take his gun.

"Sir?" Burke stood in the doorway.

Luke's first priority was his son, so he handed Burke the poker and ordered, "Make sure he's not hiding in any of the rooms on this floor." Then he continued toward the nursery, which was the next door.

The nursery looked just as it had when Luke had rescued Sally from Jeffrey's early morning high energy, telling the nurse he would take the boy to the park. Nothing looked amiss.

Luke carefully lay Jeffrey in his bed, and the child rolled onto his side and continued sleeping.

Taking the poker from the nursery fireplace, he gave it to Sally. "Watch over him, and don't hesitate to scream if you see a strange man."

"Yes, sir." The petite young woman gripped the poker with a determined look. She might have looked comical if Luke hadn't been gritting his teeth as he planned what he would do if the intruder would only show himself.

There were two other rooms on that floor. Luke

threw open the next door, which was his old bedroom. It also appeared undisturbed.

He confiscated that fireplace's poker and advanced to the only room he hadn't yet checked—the bedroom where Anne had slept. The door was ajar, and he shoved it open.

Anne's room was ransacked even more horribly than Luke's. Every drawer had been emptied on the floor. The mattress had been pulled off the bed and slashed open, along with the pillows. Her tall upright cupboard had been emptied and the back of it smashed. Her trunks were open and upended, the bottom knocked out. Clothing was everywhere, all over the floor and draped over every surface.

Luke quickly checked to make sure no one was lurking in a corner even as his stomach churned at seeing Anne's bedroom, her personal things, thrown violently about the room. He'd carefully avoided her bedroom ever since she died. It was like a punch in the gut to see it in such a state.

But this was no time for complicated sentiment. He returned to his own bedroom.

"I didn't find anyone," Burke said, still wielding the poker.

"Did no one hear anything?" Luke asked Burke in the doorway. "There should have been a lot of noise when they smashed the wooden trunks and furniture."

"I was fetching the pantry items for the day," Burke said. "When I come in the house, Cobb was at the bottom of the stairs and the maidservants was huddled around him on the floor."

"And where was Smith?"

"Smith must of been in his room in the basement,

for he comes out running, not quite fully dressed. He must of heard the women crying out."

Luke sighed. "Very well. Let's go and check the attic."

They stored unused furniture in the attic, and it was also where some of the female servants had their sleeping quarters. After a thorough search, Luke and Burke found no strange men and nothing out of place and made their way back down the stairs.

Luke remained cautious, constantly checking his surroundings, still holding the iron poker like a weapon.

He went first to the nursery, peeking in to see Sally sitting beside Jeffrey's bed. The boy was still asleep.

Luke continued down to the entry hall, still carefully looking and listening, then going down to the basement level where Cobb was being attended to by the surgeon, Mr. Pyle.

Pyle stood and bid the footmen carry Cobb to his room.

"Will he recover?" Luke asked.

"He may, if he regains consciousness," Mr. Pyle said, pressing his lips together and shaking his head. "It is hard to say with this kind of head injury. He may also have broken bones or internal wounds. We should pray that his senses are restored and he is able to tell us his symptoms."

"Yes, of course." Luke's heart sank even as heat crept into his face. How dare someone come into his home and push his butler down a flight of stairs? The rage nearly overwhelmed him.

"Send for me if he awakens." Mr. Pyle was leaving.

"Is there nothing you can do for him?" Luke felt his anger shifting toward the surgeon. "Are you leaving him to die?"

"There is nothing else that I can do." Mr. Pyle straightened his shoulders and looked Luke in the eye. "I'm sorry, sir, but his healing is in God's hands now."

Luke didn't trust himself to speak, so he gave a quick nod and turned away.

In God's hands. Wasn't that where Luke had placed his marriage?

He knew he couldn't let this bitterness gain a foothold, but he had desperately wanted to believe that things would get better, that his wife would not be unfaithful to him and show so little interest in her home and her child.

Why must he live a destroyed life instead of the normal one everyone else seemed to enjoy? Wives of English gentlemen did not behave in such a way as to bring shame upon themselves and their families. So why had his wife done that?

God, I want to pray for Cobb, for you to heal him, but . . . do you even hear me? Do you even care?

He was wrong to think such things, but he couldn't seem to stop himself. They were in his mind before he could counter them.

Mr. Pyle had departed when the scullery maid hurried over and started cleaning up what was left of the drying blood on the floor.

Who would have done this violence? Obviously they had been looking for something, focusing in on Anne's room. But what?

His mind went to Lenoir, whom he'd seen watching him in the park. Did that man have something to do with this? He couldn't have been the one who'd searched the house, but was he behind it?

Luke remembered that Henry had asked him to let

him know if Luke saw the man following him.

The two footmen, Smith and Burke, approached. "We searched the house and found no one. Should we fetch the constable?"

"No, not just yet. In fact, I will . . . will speak to the proper authority. Thank you. But I do have a task for you."

They stared expectantly.

"I want one of you to watch Jeffrey's room at all times, and the other to watch the back door until I tell you otherwise. Just as a precaution."

The men nodded. "Yes, sir."

Luke hurried from the house, barely remembering to grab his hat on the way out.

Chapter Three

When Jane entered her shop, she saw that there were new hats in the window. She admired them for a few moments before heading to the back, where she found her partner, Catherine Cosworth, speaking to a customer about the summer muslin fabric she was thinking of purchasing.

Jane caught Catherine's eye and they exchanged a quick look before Jane proceeded to the tiny room where the account books were kept.

As she sat in the chair behind the desk and reached for the ledger, she let out a long sigh of contentment. There was something so satisfying in knowing that one had a job to do, something necessary and exact, the reconciling of numbers on a page. It was a task that was precise, with a beginning and an end—and it was normally done by men.

Even more satisfying was knowing that this business belonged to Jane—half of it, leastwise—and that she was taking care of it. This sense of ownership was something she'd never before experienced, and it gave her life a sense of purpose. Someday, she predicted, more women would seek out such employment and purpose.

Jane picked up the two stacks of receipts—one for

sales and the other for purchase orders—and began to enter the numbers in the ledger.

How tidy and perfect the rows of numbers were, if she did say so herself. The clerk that Catherine had previously employed had written in such a careless hand, sometimes it was difficult for Jane to decipher what he'd recorded. But she was careful to make her pen strokes with precision. Then she would use a piece of scrap paper to add or subtract the columns of numbers before entering the sum into the ledger.

Once the numbers had been written, she would analyze them: the different purchases, the price of each, profit margins, and prepare to discuss it all with Catherine when she was not busy with a customer.

"You have a head for business, Jane," Catherine had told her more than once. "You are so good mathematically, with all the figuring and numbers, it's almost scandalous."

"Why should men be the only ones who are good at business and numbers? But you are better than I am at knowing what styles and materials to have in stock, purchasing everything at the best possible cost, and knowing the right price for things. You are the true heart and soul of the shop."

"Well, I would not even have a shop if it were not for you."

"Touché."

Jane's school friend had fallen on difficult times when her shop-owning husband had died of consumption. The couple had run the shop together, but when he was very sick and near death, the shop had done poorly, as Catherine had been unable to keep it open as much. With her husband's medical bills, by the time he passed away she was nearly destitute and looking for someone to buy the business.

"Why don't I buy half the business?" Jane had asked Catherine, after thinking it over for less than five minutes. "I have the inheritance my aunt left me, and this way we can be partners."

Catherine looked astonished. "But Jane, are you sure? People will talk. They'll say you've given up on finding a husband."

"What do I care what people say? It's none of their affair, and they should keep their noses out of other people's business, both literally and figuratively speaking."

Jane smirked and Catherine hid a laugh behind her hand.

"Besides," Jane continued, "my aunt gave me that money, and she said she didn't want me to feel as if I had no choice except to get married. She knew I'd hate marrying someone I didn't love and respect."

Aunt Madeline had not been very fortunate or happy in her own marriage. She had not been blessed with children, and Jane was a favorite of hers. Some said she and Jane were very alike.

"Better to have money and not need a husband than to marry out of necessity." Catherine stared wistfully at the wall.

Catherine understood this better than most, as her husband had left her with no money, and she'd had to sell their house to pay off their debts. She was currently sleeping in the small room above the shop. Jane had begged her to come and stay in the townhouse she shared with her brother and mother, when they were in London, but Catherine was far too independent and worried that she might inconvenience Jane's family.

"But a business is not a certainty," Catherine continued. "It is possible that the shop will do poorly and you will lose your investment."

"The shop is doing well and will continue to do so. We shall both work hard and make money hand over fist. You'll see."

Catherine laughed again and shook her head. "You are a godsend, Jane Gilchrist."

"As are you, Catherine Cosworth."

Jane had no thoughts of owning a shop until she discovered Catherine was looking for a part owner and investor, and she never imagined she'd enjoy being a shop owner so much. She'd once told Catherine, "Doing the accounts gives me something to do besides sit at home embroidering cushions."

"As if you've ever embroidered a cushion in your life." Catherine snorted, then covered her mouth with a horrified look.

Jane made no attempt to hide her laugh. "Thank the Lord I am not the only woman in England who is sometimes unladylike."

She remembered Catherine turning pink but then smiling good-naturedly. She was a sweet, shy girl—quite unlike Jane—but the two young women had always gotten along well. Catherine was certainly trustworthy, and Jane had not hesitated to go into business with her as a partner.

Besides, Jane quite liked the idea that a young, never-married woman owning a business would be considered a bit scandalous, even unfeminine, and brand her unmarriageable. But her mother and brother had both said, "It suits you."

As Jane finished up the accounts, the time having flown by as it always did when she was so occupied, Catherine came into the room with a contented smile.

"How was business today?" Jane asked as she closed the ledger.

Catherine handed over the money tray and receipts and she put them in their proper place.

"Very brisk for a Wednesday. It seems we shall have another good week."

"Thanks to your savvy sense of fashion." Jane smiled.

"You are much too complimentary of me and my fashion and business sense." Catherine shook her head.

"And you're much too modest. When someone compliments you, just say, 'Thank you.' Besides, I sincerely doubt that you've ever been given a compliment that you didn't deserve."

"Well, I shall remember your advice for the next time someone compliments me." Catherine turned aside and said, "Thank you," smirking and curtsying to an unseen bearer of compliments.

Jane laughed as she stood and prepared to leave. "We are a pair, are we not? I defy any man not to want to marry us."

Catherine shook her head again, but there was a bit of sadness in her expression, which seemed to disappear as quickly as it came.

The lamplighters were just climbing their ladders to light the streetlamps as Jane started to walk home in the waning light, until she saw that Henry had sent the carriage for her.

She was helped inside by the footman, and as she settled against the seat cushions, she thought of

Catherine, alone in her room above the shop—the poor girl. She considered different ways the two of them could make more money, enough that Catherine could get a decent place to live. Perhaps they could open another shop, even expand to other towns like Bath. She would have to put in some time planning their expansion.

When she arrived home, Jane was greeted by a servant. "Mr. Gilchrist and Mr. Watley are waiting for you in the sitting room."

Mr. Luke Watley? What was he doing there?

Jane took off her bonnet and gloves and went into the sitting room, where Henry and Luke Watley both stood to greet her, looking quite somber.

"Jane, you know Mr. Luke Watley," Henry said.

"Yes, of course. We spoke this morning in the park."

"Mr. Watley and I have reason to believe that a man with evil intent followed him and his son into the park and that he made note of your interaction with them."

"I don't understand. A man with evil intent?"

Henry hesitated, glancing at Mr. Watley.

"Miss Gilchrist," Mr. Watley said, his jaw flexing, "my home was ransacked today while my son and I were at the park, and my butler was seriously injured by the intruder."

"Oh no! Is your butler all right? What I mean to say is, will he recover?"

"He has not regained consciousness. We have consulted a surgeon and a physician and neither of them know if he ever will." The man's breath seemed to leave him as he said the words, his shoulders sagging. He took a sip from the glass in his hand, as if to distract himself.

"I am terribly sorry. That is most dreadful." Truly, she felt a bit sick at the thought of such violence on an innocent servant. She imagined how she would feel if such a thing happened to their butler, and she wished she could punish that intruder herself.

"I was concerned," Mr. Watley said, clearing his throat, "that you might be in danger. He might think you and I have a closer association than we actually do."

"But why is the man so dangerous, and why does he mean you harm, if I may ask?" But as soon as she said the words Jane wished she could take them back, for this must undoubtedly have to do with Mr. Watley's wife and the rumors about her unfaithfulness.

"He is a revolutionary," Henry said, "intent on overthrowing Britain's monarchy. His name is Lenoir."

Mr. Watley did not meet her gaze as he said in a wry tone, his bottom lip curling, "He was an associate of my wife's. It seems likely that he thinks she has hidden something incriminating in my house."

"Oh, I'm sorry. Is Jeffrey safe?"

"I have just returned from taking Jeffrey to my home in the country. It is only a half day's ride in the carriage from London, but I thought he'd be safer there."

"I told Mr. Watley that I thought you were safe, that it's unlikely Lenoir will bother you," Henry said. "But he wanted to make sure you knew the man was dangerous."

"What does he look like, this Lenoir?" She tried to recall the few men she had seen in the park that morning.

"He has dark hair and eyes and a black mustache and a beard that is small and comes to a point." Henry used his hand to indicate a short beard that came just below his chin.

"I do recall seeing a man of that description." Jane remembered exactly where he'd been standing, but her memories of his face were indistinct. "Was he thin, with a narrow face?"

"Yes, that is him," Henry said.

Mr. Watley looked a bit pale as he took another sip of his drink. The poor man. Lenoir had been rumored to be his wife's paramour, but even worse if she was involved with revolutionaries. No one wanted a repeat of what had so recently happened in France.

Well, that was not entirely true. There were people who would love to see an overthrow of Great Britain's government, much as France's had been violently overthrown and their monarchy executed.

"Truthfully, anyone who was a close friend of the late Mrs. Watley is probably in more danger than you are," Henry said. "But better to be safe than sorry. We both think you should take every precaution and, at the very least, not go on any more solitary walks for a while."

"I could not live with myself if you were injured because of me, Miss Gilchrist." Mr. Watley's face was stoic now, his jaw and mouth set in hard lines.

Men did not like showing emotion. But she understood. Jane herself was quite careful not to show a lot of emotion in public. It was not an acceptable practice, according to Society rules and norms.

"I thank you for your concern for my welfare," Jane said. "I shall take care to not be alone, and I'm sure I shall be well." She was suddenly struck with how thoughtful and courteous it was of Mr. Watley to be so concerned for her safety. Most men in the same situation would not have put themselves out in such a way, especially when it had to do with an unfaithful wife. Such humiliation must be quite difficult to bear.

"Mr. Watley and I have a few more things to talk about, if you wish to go," Henry said quietly.

Jane nodded to them and left the room.

Could it be that Mr. Watley was such an exceptional man? Or was there a reason, some sort of fault of his, that had put him in his present predicament? Though it seemed unkind to lay any blame, she didn't like that she was suddenly so wont to think well of Mr. Watley. It felt safer to think ill of him.

She remembered how he'd been surrounded by young unmarried ladies at the ball a couple of nights ago, and she'd indulged in feelings of contempt for him, so newly widowed, enjoying so much attention. It was easier—safer, as she'd already acknowledged—to think of him that way than to realize how unselfish he was to come and warn her of danger while exposing himself to ridicule by bringing attention to the behavior of his first wife.

Surely nothing would come of it. She did regret, however, that the adorable little boy who had begged her to play with him was no longer in London and there was no chance of her seeing him again, at least for a while.

Chapter Four

Luke sighed and rubbed his chin, once again staring out the window at the streetlights.

Henry Gilchrist, who was a Member of Parliament and the head of a committee that investigated threats to the country and the monarchy, had installed two soldiers at Luke's home to make sure everyone in the household was safe from nefarious intruders. Henry was concerned that the attacker might decide to come back to finish off Cobb so that he couldn't identify him.

Cobb was in bed, unconscious but still breathing. The physician and surgeon agreed that it was probably best he not be moved, and he needed watching over.

Would this nightmare never end? The servants had done their best to clean the rooms—all but Anne's, which Luke purposely left as it was when it was ransacked. Henry would send someone to help him go through the room and carefully look, in case the intruder had missed something. But Luke was left with many feelings, including rage at the intruder, rage at Lenoir, and wave after wave of sadness.

God, where are you?
I will never leave you nor forsake you.
He felt comforted by the words, even as he

struggled to understand them. With a sigh, he determined to get his thoughts off these emotions that threatened to tear him in two. There had to be a clear path forward, and he had to get control of his emotions. He couldn't go his whole life being angry with God and angry with his wife—she was dead, for heaven's sake.

Luke sighed again and ran his hand through his hair. Forgiveness seemed the key to peace of mind, and he had to forgive because God required it. But how could he forgive people who weren't sorry and didn't acknowledge what they had done to him? How was that even possible? His mind and heart both rebelled.

Of course, in moments like this, he had to reflect on the fact that God had forgiven him of every careless word, thought, and action, all of his outright sins, and that was one reason he must forgive each person who wronged him, including Anne and Lenoir.

People had told him that it would get easier. Perhaps that was what he should focus his thoughts on —that the passing of time would eventually make this all less painful.

His first reaction was to hold onto anger and pride, and he'd even lashed out at a few people who had only been trying to help him. But for Jeffrey's sake he had to let go of the anger and pride. Jeffrey now had no other close family. Luke's parents and most of his family were gone. He'd never had siblings, and at the moment he felt that those who were from large families were the fortunate ones. He felt so alone.

Once again, he began to wonder if remarrying was the answer to his pain. If he could remarry, have more children, he wouldn't feel alone. He could crowd out the pain and bad memories with happiness and hope. And once again, it wasn't so much his own wisdom and rational thinking that stopped him from that path. It was his fear, the fear that he might marry another woman like Anne who would rip his heart out and trample on his self-respect, who would be unfaithful and humiliate him. And he could not endure that again.

Was there something wrong with him? Was he not man enough for the kind of woman he wanted? Perhaps, instead of marrying an intelligent woman with ideas and opinions of her own, a strong-willed woman—which was the kind of woman he'd always been attracted to —he should marry a gentle, quiet, unassuming woman, someone who would say yes to anything he suggested, who would never wish to travel without him or do anything other than stay home and manage their children and household.

Such a woman did not particularly appeal to him, but he was certain that she was exactly what he needed and was the key to his happiness. He had married someone he was attracted to, but next time he would marry sensibly.

If he was honest, when he watched Jane Gilchrist playing with Jeffrey in the park that morning, his heart had nearly leapt out of his chest. How kind and playful she was, giving Jeffrey her undivided attention, making him smile and laugh more than even Luke was able to make him laugh lately.

In those moments, he had been very drawn to Jane, had thought her the prettiest woman he'd ever seen— the way she smiled and the artless way she played with Jeffrey. But she was not quiet or unassuming. He'd even heard a rumor that she was part owner of a shop in London. Besides that, she'd never shown any interest in him, either before he married Anne nor since her death, and he would not marry another woman who didn't love or care for him.

Luke would be wise this time. He would choose a woman who was docile and accommodating, who gave him all her attention, even if he didn't feel particularly attracted to her. Attraction could not be important when choosing a wife, because he had been very attracted to Anne, and he saw how that had turned out.

But at this point in his life, he wasn't sure he would be able to trust even a quiet and compliant woman enough to marry her. What if she changed once they were married?

No, he wasn't ready to marry. He would focus on taking care of Jeffrey. The poor child had no mother, but Luke was determined to be both mother and father to him, to give him whatever he needed. Luke knew what it was like to be an orphan, and the last thing he wanted was for his son to suffer.

Or to marry another faithless, troubled, troublesome woman.

~ ~ ~

Jane awakened during the night. She tried to go back to sleep but her thoughts were full of Luke Watley and all that he and his son had been through. It seemed strange, but she couldn't seem to get Luk's face out of her mind—the way he had looked when he was warning her about the small chance that she might be in danger, the sadness in his eyes. He looked as if he had not been sleeping very well either.

She got up and poured herself a glass of water, taking a sip as she went to the window. She didn't bother to light a candle. She was familiar enough with her room, and there was enough light from the streetlamps.

As she gazed down at the street below, she noticed a bit of movement. As she stared, she could make out two men standing under the lamp below, and they were both gazing up at her house.

Jane drew in a quick breath and froze, then took a small step back away from the window. She didn't think they could see her, as there was no light behind her, but they seemed to be staring at her window—definitely at the house. As she continued to stare down at them, she realized one of the men was the man with the pointed beard from the park, Lenoir.

The men did not seem alarmed, so she was fairly certain they didn't see her in the window. Then they both started toward the house and disappeared below, out of her line of vision.

What were they doing? Were they breaking into the house as Mr. Watley's intruder had done?

Jane kept a heavy iron candlestick by her bed, and part of her wanted to defend herself with it, but she felt it was wiser to go and inform her brother.

She ran in her bare feet from her room to her brother's room and knocked on the door.

"Who is it?" his voice called out.

"Jane," she said, trying not to speak too loudly, as she didn't want to wake her sister-in-law Penelope or their sleeping baby, Lilith.

A few moments later Henry came out, shutting the door behind him, and finished donning his robe.

"I saw Lenoir and another man on the street staring up at the house," Jane said in a loud whisper. "Then they came toward the house and I lost sight of them."

"Come with me." Henry hurried down the hall. His

hand was in the pocket of his robe, and when he pulled his hand out he was holding a pistol.

At the head of the stairs they found the new footman sitting in a chair propped against the wall, asleep.

"Get up," Henry said, nudging the man's shoulder.

The man awoke with a sharp intake of breath, shooting out of the chair to his feet.

"Go check the back door. If you see anything suspicious, call the other servants to arm themselves. But if you don't see anything, come back to Miss Gilchrist's room."

"Yes, sir." The man hurried down the stairs, looking wide awake.

They headed back to Jane's room. Just as they opened the door, Jane heard the sound of breaking glass. A man was in the window, his hand coming through to unlock and open it.

Henry used his arm to push Jane behind him. He was pointing his gun at the man but didn't say a word, as if waiting to see what he would do.

The man yanked the window open and tumbled into the room.

Henry raced across the room and struck him in the head with the butt of his pistol. The man fell over and lay unmoving on the floor.

Just behind him, a second man appeared in the window, but he stopped, as if standing on a ladder. He seemed to be peering into the room, but Jane couldn't tell because all the light was behind him, keeping his face dark.

Henry struck the man in the face with his fist. The man threw his hands forward, trying to catch onto something to stop his backward fall.

Henry grabbed him by the arm and hauled him into the room, throwing him face down before stomping on the back of the man's neck.

"I have a gun trained on your head. I will shoot you." Henry's voice was barely recognizable, so cold and gruff as it was.

The next thing Jane knew, the two men were scrambling on the floor, then a gunshot rang out—so loud it seemed to make Jane go deaf.

She ran forward to help Henry, but it was the man on the floor who was moaning and making distressed noises in his throat.

"Fetch a candle," Henry said, now holding two guns, both trained on the men.

Jane hurried out of the room just before hearing several voices calling out, including servants from downstairs and Penelope's from down the hall.

Jane called, a bubble of excitement in her chest, "Your master has caught two intruders." She hurried into Penelope's room, which she shared—scandalously—with Henry. "May I have the lantern from Lilith's room?" Jane knew Penelope kept a lantern in the small adjoining room where the baby slept.

"Of course." Penelope was already out of bed and in her robe as she hurried with Jane into Lilith's room. She quickly turned up the flame and handed it to Jane, who ran to her own room.

The lantern illuminated her brother, still standing over the two men on the floor. Both of the men were moaning now, with a dark blood stain on the shoulder of one of them.

Servants appeared in the doorway and Henry

rapidly gave orders, sending one servant to fetch the constable, one for the surgeon, and one to fetch rope. Soon they were tying the intruders' hands behind them, then rolling them over onto their backs.

Jane brought the lantern close to their faces but neither one of them was Lenoir.

"Smith," Henry said, looking up at one of the footmen. "Go out onto the street and look for a man with a small black beard standing about. And take someone with you."

"Yes, sir."

Jane was glad to see that Smith was armed with a fire poker.

Penelope was now standing in the doorway. "Is everyone all right?" she asked.

"All is well, darling," Henry said. "You may go back to bed. I'll be there as soon as I can."

The sound of a baby crying came from the nearby room.

"Shall I check on Lilith?" Jane asked, but Penelope was already turning to go.

"I shall see to her," Penelope said. "Thank you, Jane. But you may come with me, if you like."

Jane decided to leave the bloody, moaning captives to her brother and the servants and went with her sister-in-law.

Lilith was being held and soothed by the nurse when the two of them entered the room.

"I heard a loud noise," the young nurse said. "Is everything all right?"

"Yes, all is well," Penelope said with a smile, as if there weren't two frightening men down the hall who were bent on some errand of evil. She took the baby from the nurse's arms and kissed her cheek. "There, there," Penelope soothed. "Did you hear strange noises while you were trying to sleep? Poor dear."

Penelope had such faith in Henry that she didn't worry, even when their house had been intruded upon. Finally, as Lilith quieted, she whispered, "Are you all right, Jane?"

"Oh, yes, I am well. Henry caught the men as they crawled through the window." Thinking of the sight of them flopping in, never suspecting that Henry was waiting for them, almost made her laugh. But when she remembered how Henry had hit the one man so ruthlessly, and shot the other when he must have been reaching for Henry's gun, her stomach sank and a shiver went across her shoulders.

Of course, she was grateful for how Henry had apprehended the men. The viciousness was necessary to defend them all from the intruders who, after all, were carrying guns and obviously intent on evil. Yet it was unnerving to see it happen in front of her.

She thought of the candlestick beside her bed. What if she had not been awake and had not looked out the window when she did? What if she'd been asleep in her bed when the men had come in through her window?

She only hoped she would have awakened in time to grab her candlestick and bash them in the head. But one of them obviously had a gun. Would they have kidnapped her, taking her for ransom? It was all quite terrifying, even if she didn't feel very frightened.

She imagined herself successfully doing battle with the two men. It helped her peace of mind to imagine it.

Could this have happened because of that man,

Lenoir, seeing her interacting with Luke Watley and his son in the park? Or did it have more to do with Henry and his work with the committee that kept track of secret societies that were aligned against the government and the monarchy?

Either way, she would not let anyone intimidate her. It was not in her nature to shrink from a fight.

However, it was not in her mother's nature to fight. So Jane would write to her mother, warning her not to come to London just yet, not until they were able to capture Lenoir and thwart his plans.

Chapter Five

Luke slept very little these days, so it was no wonder he was awake when an urgent message arrived from Henry Gilchrist saying that two men had broken into his house, coming through his sister Jane's window armed with pistols. She had seen Lenoir outside just before it happened.

Heat crawled up the back of his neck as he read the message. Finally he saw the words, "Jane and everyone else in the house are well and unharmed." The note ended with, "One intruder was knocked unconscious and the other was shot, but both are expected to recover."

Perhaps they would get some answers from the men about what Lenoir wanted and what his plans were.

Poor Jane Gilchrist. He hated to think that her kindness to little Jeffrey had put her in danger. It seemed likely the men were intent on kidnapping her. What else could it be? They couldn't think there was something important hidden in her room, as she had nothing to do with Anne or the group that wanted to overthrow the government. And Lenoir was no petty thief. But now that they had captured Lenoir's two henchmen, Henry could possibly find out from his henchmen what Lenoir was looking for when he ransacked Luke's home.

As soon as he was able to get dressed and ready, Luke went to Henry's house.

He was led into the drawing room where Henry was meeting with several men—another Member of Parliament as well as a few rough-looking men.

"Forgive me for interrupting," Luke said.

"We are just finishing," Henry said, as the men began to depart.

When they were gone, Henry turned to Luke. "I hope my early morning note did not disturb you. You haven't had any trouble there, have you?"

"No, no trouble. Cobb is still breathing but has not awakened."

"Yes, I know," Henry mumbled grimly.

Luke started to ask him how he knew, but it occurred to him that the guards he had sent to watch over Cobb would report to Henry.

"What can I do?" Luke asked his friend. "How can I help? You must give me a task."

Henry's brow wrinkled slightly, as if he was thinking. "I don't know that you can help, since Lenoir obviously knows what you look like and who you are."

"I at least need to know what it is Lenoir was searching for in my house."

"If we can get it out of the two men we captured, I will personally let you know."

Luke ran his hand through his hair. This anger and frustration was almost overwhelming. "You will tell me if there is something I can do?"

"Of course. I know it must be difficult, but try to put it out of your mind. Perhaps you should join your son in Hertfordshire."

"No, I have business in London. Besides . . ." Luke

sighed as he made an effort to shove down his feelings. "I want to be here in case there is something I can do."

Sometimes he wondered if he was just punishing himself for some unknown reason. Perhaps it was because he felt responsible for his wife—what husband wouldn't?—and now she was dead, possibly murdered.

"Try to get some rest," Henry said, compassion in his expression. "And it is all right if you return to your country house. We will do what is necessary here in London, and I will keep you informed."

"I know, I know. But . . . I cannot leave just yet."

"Very well." Henry laid a hand on his shoulder. "Do try to sleep. Your son needs you to stay well."

"Of course." As he turned to leave, he asked, "And your sister, Miss Gilchrist? Is she well after the shock of last night?"

"She is well." A slight smile appeared on Henry's face. "Jane is a girl who prides herself on not being like other girls and rather enjoys danger. She's probably regretting that she went to tell me she saw Lenoir out her window, wishing she could have shot the men herself." Henry was still smiling.

She sounded a bit like Anne, which didn't exactly endear Miss Gilchrist to him.

"I am glad Miss Gilchrist was unharmed," was all Luke allowed himself to say.

"Thank you. And do come to our ball tomorrow night. Penelope doesn't give a lot of parties, but she highly anticipates the ones she does give."

"Of course. If I am feeling up to it."

"Come even if you don't feel up to it," Henry said. "We will lift your spirits, or at least we will distract you for a few hours."

"I will." Luke committed himself, since he might learn something from Henry about Lenoir and his men, their motives and goals. Besides, Jeffrey would be in bed asleep by the time he left for the ball, and those early hours right after dark were the loneliest.

~ ~ ~

Luke's business in London was to settle Anne's debts. It must be done, as depressing a task as it was, and he had decided to do it himself rather than sending his solicitor. Gossip surrounding his wife was rampant enough, and the less people knew of her affairs the better.

So, two hours after meeting with Henry Gilchrist, he set out with a list of creditors.

The first shop on the list was not too far away. He arrived and went inside. There were two customers, and the one shop attendant was busy assisting them.

Luke pretended to look around while he waited, glancing at the bonnets and parasols on display and at the fabric and dresses. Soon his mind wandered, his thoughts leading him back—as always—to painful memories, until he wasn't even seeing the goods in front of his eyes.

"May I help—oh, it's you, Mr. Watley."

He turned toward the voice and found Jane Gilchrist standing in front of him.

"How may I help you?" she asked, squinting slightly as she gazed at him.

"Oh, I just need to settle my wife's account with the shopkeeper." He felt his face start to heat up. Why was Miss Gilchrist asking if she could help him?

"Well, I am the shop's half owner and bookkeeper. I can help you with that. I saw that Catherine was busy with other customers and didn't want you to wait too long."

"So the rumor was true," Luke said, "that you are an owner in a shop."

"Yes, I'm afraid I truly am a woman scandalous enough to go into business."

"Forgive me. I didn't mean to insinuate—that is, I don't consider a woman engaged in business to be scandalous." No, what his wife had done was a much better definition of "scandalous." But he was aware that many people of the upper levels of Society would consider her involvement in the shop to be improper for a lady of her station.

She smiled. "Please wait here while I find Mrs. Watley's account and give you the total."

"Thank you, Miss Gilchrist."

Luke watched her walk to the back of the shop and disappear through a doorway.

She was a lady, with a family who cared for her, a large country home in Hertfordshire, and a townhouse in a fashionable part of London. She didn't need to work as a bookkeeper or own a shop. She could do what other young ladies did and spend her time reading, visiting, practicing on the pianoforte, shopping, embroidering, and planning what she would wear to the next party.

She was intriguing, he had to admit. But he would do well to remember that he planned to marry someone who was quiet and docile, when he did decide to marry again. As for Miss Gilchrist, some would say she engaged in "manly pursuits." Certainly, she did not fit his idea of a woman who was content to stay at home. And though she intrigued him, he would be polite and treat her as he would any other young lady, but he was much too aware of Jane's similarity to Anne, who was never satisfied to stay at home.

Anne had once told him, "I'm restless. You can't expect a restless, active soul like mine to just sit and do nothing, and I despise embroidery and playing instruments. I shall go to London or I shall die."

His stomach churned as he remembered her dramatic declaration, which was actually a threat. She knew he cared about her and that he wanted her to be an attentive mother to Jeffrey. So telling him she would die if she didn't get her way . . .

She was a troubled woman, so much more troubled than he had realized when he married her. She'd fooled him before they were wed into thinking she was a steady, loving, even shy and docile young woman who happened to be orphaned, like him. He had thought her the most beguiling creature he'd ever met. But after they were wed, she became a restless, mercurial threat to his own sanity, determined to spend all her time in London, her thoughts set on parties and balls and the latest gossip, all while ignoring the fact that she had a husband and a child.

He took a deep breath as more women entered the shop and stared curiously at him.

He had to stop living in the past. He was here in this shop, paying off bills, and he would not allow himself to think of anything else.

Miss Gilchrist emerged from the back room and motioned to him. He followed her into the tiny room.

"Here are your receipts." She handed him a stack of paper. "And this is your total." She pointed to a number on the paper that lay on top, with a long row of figures and the sum at the bottom.

She allowed him to sit at what must be her desk so that he could write the note to his bank. As he wrote, he marveled that a lady would choose to sit in this gloomy room and add and subtract numbers all day and write them in ledgers. And although Miss Gilchrist's independent spirit had at times reminded him of Anne, her work in this shop certainly did not.

He stood and handed her the note.

"Thank you," she said.

He imagined Miss Gilchrist was feeling sorry for him, thinking of how he had married a woman who would spend his money and then be unfaithful to him.

"I hope I shall see you at our ball tonight," she said. "Penelope and Henry are looking forward to seeing you, I know."

"I told Henry I would try to be there. And I hope you are no worse for what happened last night. You certainly look well."

"Thank you. It was a shock, of course, but I was not hurt." She smiled as if it was nothing. "I believe Henry and the other brave men helping him will get all of the ones bent on destroying our country and put them in prison so that no one else will be hurt."

Like Anne. She had been killed by these men.

"It is an unfortunate business," Luke said. "I wouldn't want anyone else to be hurt either. If anyone can stop them, it is Henry." Desperate to change the subject, he said, "So this is your shop?"

"Yes. Well, my friend Catherine owned the shop with her husband, but when he died he left her with a lot of debt, so I offered to buy out half of the business and help her with the accounts. This freed her up to wait on customers so she doesn't have to pay anyone to mind the shop, and I do the bookkeeping."

"That is quite generous and kind of you, Miss Gilchrist."

"It works out well for both of us. The shop is making money, and I find I quite enjoy keeping the books."

"You enjoy it? Sitting here in this little office?"

"I do." She folded her arms in front of her chest, giving him a challenging look. "I enjoy seeing the numbers line up and reconcile. It is satisfying for me. But I see this surprises you. Do you think a woman cannot enjoy mathematics and accounting?"

"I hope I have not offended you. I just find it . . . unusual."

"Perhaps it is. But I dislike sitting at home embroidering cushions."

Heat crept up the back of his neck. Hadn't Anne said almost those exact words to him, more than once? And Luke wanted no part of a woman who was like Anne —faithless, restless, cruel.

"I see. Good day, Miss Gilchrist." He turned to leave, knowing he was being abrupt, but his breath was coming fast and he just needed to leave.

"Good day, Mr. Watley. Thank you for settling your wife's bill."

"I must go. Thank you."

Was she mentioning his wife purposely to bother him? No, he was being paranoid, as he often was when something reminded him of Anne.

But his visceral reaction was further proof that anyone who reminded him of Anne was not someone he would ever marry.

~ ~ ~

Jane hurried home from the shop to get ready for the ball. When she entered the house, her brother and sister-in-law were standing in the hallway locked in an amorous embrace.

They must have heard her shut the door, because they immediately stopped kissing. Penelope broke into an embarrassed laugh, while Henry just smiled and greeted Jane.

Truly, she wished she could have what Henry and Penelope had—a sincerely loving and affectionate marriage. But such a thing seemed so rare.

There were many spinsters in England, and she might well end up as one of them, as she would not accept anything less than a man she could love and respect.

"Don't mind me," Jane said. "Your secret—that you have an affectionate marriage—is safe with me."

"We aren't the only couple in England with an affectionate marriage," Henry said.

"You are the only one I know of." Jane raised her eyebrows, daring him to dispute it.

Henry changed the subject. "Are you excited for the ball this evening? I know how much you like to dance."

"Of course. And if the popular Mr. Luke Watley is in attendance, I daresay I shall have the pick of dance partners, as every young lady will be trying to dance with him."

Henry shook his head. "Why do you dislike him so much?"

"I don't dislike him." Jane frowned at her irritating brother, always so quick to scold her.

"I feel so sorry for poor Mr. Watley," Penelope said. "I do hope he comes and that we can cheer him up a bit. He looks so sad every time I see him, and now he's had to send his sweet little boy to the country just to keep him safe." Penelope looked as if she had tears in her eyes, but she blinked them away.

Jane wanted to roll her eyes, if she was honest, at how much pity Luke Watley was receiving. "I saw him this morning. He is well enough. He is sought after by every young lady and her mother in the whole of Great Britain. He's wealthy. He can literally marry any woman he wants. In a few months he'll be better than ever, I daresay."

"Jane." Penelope's eyes went wide and she shook her head. "You are just trying to be shocking." She smiled as if amused.

"Really, Jane. That isn't very charitable," Henry said. "The man has suffered a great deal. You cannot dispute the point."

"I know. The man has suffered, but it isn't as if he is penniless and in need, as is the case with many women who are widowed, or that he will never marry again. His situation will change and be quite well again. That is all I am saying."

She also remembered how abrupt he had been with her that morning. Was he thinking about how scandalous and "masculine" it was that she enjoyed working? After all, she'd just told him how much she liked keeping the accounts. Why else would he have been uncivil in the way he took his leave?

"Do be kind to him tonight, my dear," Penelope said, a crease forming above the bridge of her nose.

"Am I not always kind?" Jane waved her hand. "Don't worry. I will not abuse the gentleman with whom every other unmarried lady in London is in love."

Penelope smiled indulgently while Henry frowned at her. She hurried past them. "I must get dressed for tonight."

Why *did* she resent all the attention and pity Luke

Watley was getting? Perhaps it was because it was his own fault he married unwisely. Or perhaps she wished Society would give as much sympathy and compassion to poor widows as they did to poor Mr. Watley. After all, men didn't crowd around Penelope, vying for her attention, when her first husband died and left her penniless, his estate entailed upon a cousin. Nor did anyone express great sympathy and concern for Catherine when her husband died and left her in debt.

Perhaps she was also comparing herself to him, that her chances at a good marriage were much inferior to his. But this kind of thinking smacked of pettiness and envy, two horribly unkind traits. With a sinking feeling, she wondered if Henry was right about her when he said she wasn't very charitable.

As Penelope and Henry were so eager for her to be kind to Mr. Watley, she was determined to be so, for their sake. But she would not allow anyone to accuse her of throwing herself at him, of pursuing the young widower. She would be as friendly to him as to the other marriageable gentlemen present.

Chapter Six

Luke rode through the nighttime streets toward the assembly rooms the Gilchrists had rented for the ball.

He was not looking forward to an evening of trying to make pleasant conversation with people he barely knew. But perhaps it would distract him, as Henry had said. After his rather trying day of paying off all his wife's debts, getting looks of both pity and mild derision, he needed a distraction. Besides, Jeffrey was away in Hertfordshire and he had little else to occupy his time. But now that he was done with his business, he might just close up the town house tomorrow and return to Hertfordshire himself.

Let Lenoir and his men have whatever was inside. He hardly cared anymore. He'd take his servants back with him so they would be safe, and Henry might even be able to use the house as a trap to catch Lenoir.

The assembly rooms were all lit up when Luke finally arrived. Henry and his wife greeted him as soon as he walked in. And then he noticed Jane Gilchrist standing beside Mrs. Gilchrist.

She greeted him much less warmly than her brother and sister-in-law, but he hardly minded. He recalled how he had abruptly turned away from her earlier that day. But she had never seemed very eager to talk to him.

Perhaps she was one of those women who didn't care to marry. Such a thing seemed likely, since she was content to work in a shop and actually professed to enjoy it.

But then he saw the giggling, overly eager Miss Milicent Trotworthy hurrying toward him and groaned inwardly. He wasn't sure if he could stand to have her stroke his arm as she had done the last time he'd found himself at a party with her, while she crooned under her breath, "I am so sorry for what you have endured, Mr. Watley. You didn't deserve such things, and to be a widower at such a young age." Her eyes were as big as saucers, until she started blinking rapidly, as if she was about to cry.

He'd been hard-pressed to escape her, however, since several other ladies had quickly surrounded him and Miss Milicent, which brought on a pouty expression on that lady's face well worthy of a spoiled only child.

He turned to Jane and said, "May I have the first dance, Miss Gilchrist?"

Before Jane could answer him, a young gentleman who had entered the room just behind him grabbed her hand.

"Miss Gilchrist, it is the greatest pleasure to see you again. Won't you dance the first two dances with me?"

"Mr. Showalter." Jane looked almost panicked as she extricated her hand from his. She cast her eyes toward Luke and said, "I believe I am engaged to dance with Mr. Watley for those dances." She smiled apologetically at Mr. Showalter.

Just then, Miss Milicent Trotworthy's eye grew

big and her mouth fell open. She almost immediately narrowed her eyes as she stared at Jane, her jaw hardening.

"Miss Milicent, do you know Mr. Showalter?" Luke said quickly.

"I don't believe so," Milicent said, her attention all on Luke.

He introduced the two of them, even though he couldn't remember Mr. Showalter's Christian name. But Milicent barely gave Mr. Showalter a glance and acknowledged him with only a mumbled, "How do you do?"

"Mr. Watley, I was hoping . . ." Milicent started to sidle up to him.

"Would you excuse me?" Luke said quickly. "I see someone I need to speak to." He hurried away from the girl who not only wore her feelings on her sleeve, but displayed them very obviously on her face. And just now she looked as if she might stomp her foot on the floor, as her bottom lip was already beginning to protrude.

Perhaps it wasn't so gentlemanly of him to avoid the lady in such a manner. Certainly he hadn't expected to be dancing one dance, much less the first two dances, with Jane Gilchrist, but she was using him to avoid Mr. Showalter as much as he was using her to avoid Milicent.

At least Jane Gilchrist didn't seem any more interested in forming an attachment to him than he was in her.

He caught up with one of the other men on Henry's committee that watched and reported on the secret societies that had been forming in England, secret groups bent on changing England's government as France had changed theirs.

As Luke struck up a conversation with the Member of Parliament, he was glad to see that Mr. Showalter and Miss Trotworthy were getting acquainted. She soon handed him her dance card and he, no doubt, wrote his name on it, claiming a couple of dances for the evening.

Perfect.

But he wondered what Jane would think of having to dance the first two dances with him. As headstrong as she seemed to be, she might even decide she could only suffer to dance with him once. If she did, he might have to hide out in the room where the older men would be smoking and playing at cards for the second dance.

Perhaps that sounded cowardly, but he wasn't in the mood to deal with the way Miss Trotworthy always found an opportunity to touch him unnecessarily.

Would he forever be averse to another woman's touch? But it was too soon to come to that conclusion. Anne had been gone only three months.

He actually felt a little nervous at the thought of claiming the first dance with Miss Jane Gilchrist. He wasn't sure why that should be, other than the fact that she was very pretty, he always felt so drawn to her, and when he was with her he always ended up warning himself that she was not the type of woman he intended to marry.

~ ~ ~

Jane seemed to have a small bird in her stomach, fluttering its wings, when she thought of how she had committed to dancing the first two dances with Mr. Luke Watley—how she had committed him to two when he had asked her for only one dance.

How had it happened?

He'd asked her to dance the first dance with him,

but she suspected he was just trying to escape that silly Milicent Trotworthy, who was the most flirtatious woman Jane had ever encountered, and that was saying a lot. And then, in desperation, Jane had told that overeager Mr. Showalter, when he boldly asked to dance the first two dances with her, that she was engaged to dance those dances with Mr. Watley. Which wasn't strictly true.

What did Mr. Watley think of her? And what would everyone at the ball think when she danced the first two dances with him?

She knew what they would think. They would whisper about her, especially Sarah, that she was afraid of ending up a spinster and was setting her sights on poor Mr. Watley.

Why was she so mortified at that thought? She'd never thought of herself as someone who cared what other people thought of her. But obviously, she did care. She was so afraid of what they would say about her that she was contemplating how to get out of dancing the second dance.

But in reality, she very much wanted to dance with him. And that, perhaps, surprised her more than anything.

"Are you all right, my dear?" Penelope whispered next to her as they stood receiving the guests.

"Yes, of course. Why do you ask?"

"You seem a bit agitated. But you look very pretty, the prettiest woman in the room."

"You are so kind, Penelope." She almost laughed at her sweet sister-in-law. Though she was so kind, she was never insincere; she truly meant all the things she said, which was quite remarkable to Jane.

How fortunate Henry was in his choice of wife, and

Penelope was fortunate to have Henry. Jane sometimes wondered if she would ever find anyone as good as her brother; she feared she did not deserve someone that good, since she herself could be snide and critical, especially in her thoughts, and she was quite stubborn and liked her independence, more than was proper.

But she couldn't think about those things now, as she and Penelope welcomed the next guest.

Soon it was time for the first dance. Luke Watley was walking toward her, causing the fluttering wings to return. Jane did her best to dispel them and took Mr. Watley's hand, letting him lead her to the dance floor.

She gazed into his eyes. She'd never noticed how blue they were. What was he thinking as he gazed back at her? She wished she could read his thoughts, as his expression was gentle and reminded her of the way he had looked at Jeffrey when he picked the child up and held him.

What a strange thought! She could not allow herself to be as beguiled as all the other young ladies. But she had to admit, there was something incredibly romantic about him, a heartbroken widower with a small child.

Oh my! I'm as bad as the rest of them.

The music started and they began to dance.

Mr. Watley's eyes stayed focused on her, and she in turn couldn't seem to take her eyes off him. She wasn't sure she'd ever had this feeling before, as if she were perfectly in tune with him, and an unfamiliar emotion filled her chest.

She paid no attention to the other dancers, and indeed, did not even know who else was on the dance floor. The music itself seemed to carry her through the steps without her having to think about where to place a foot. And she saw only his face, imagining what he was thinking and feeling.

What had his first marriage been like? Was his heart open to loving again? After all, it was so soon. How soon was too soon? If she married him, would he open up to her about his feelings? Would theirs be an affectionate marriage, like Penelope and Henry's?

Was this how other young ladies felt when they danced with Luke Watley?

It's only a dance, it's only a dance.

She should remember that they were both using each other to avoid dancing with someone else.

Perhaps that was all it was to him. But the look in his blue eyes told her otherwise.

When had she become such a romantic? And why did she think she could read this man's thoughts?

But she was enjoying this—the dance, the way he was looking at her, the gentle but firm touch of his hand. In the back of her mind, she knew the other guests were probably watching them, jealous and whispering about Jane, the spinster who prided herself on never making her feelings for a man plain, and Luke, the wealthy young widower.

But why should she care? Those people had nothing to do with her happiness. Henry and Penelope would be watching them with completely different feelings. They wanted Jane to be happy, and they probably hoped she and Luke would make a match. Jane did not have to let that affect her feelings either, but she was genuinely captivated by Luke Watley's eyes, his handsome features, and she would not be ashamed of enjoying dancing with him.

"You look very pretty tonight," he said, as they drew near, then moved away, obeying the music and the movements of the dance.

"I thank you," she said, smiling.

Gentlemen often complimented her appearance, so she was surprised at how his words seemed to fill up her lungs until she was floating across the floor.

She never knew she could feel this way. It was a bit overwhelming.

When the dance ended, Mr. Watley offered his arm and walked her to where Penelope and Henry were talking with newly-arrived guests. He leaned down and said quietly, "I wanted to apologize for parting from you so abruptly at your shop earlier today. I have no excuse except that I was being assaulted by a bad memory. I am afraid that happens to me rather frequently these days. Forgive me for my rudeness."

"There is nothing to forgive. Politeness, especially the extreme rules of politeness, can be a burden sometimes. Truly, there is nothing to forgive."

He looked surprised, his mouth open, his eyes squinting slightly at her. "I've never heard anyone say anything like that before, but you are right. The forced politeness can be a bit of a burden. But I think you would agree that a society without politeness would also be a burden."

"Of course. Rudeness is bad, but we should all give each other more grace and stop trying to adhere to so many rules that make little sense."

He looked as if he might actually laugh. Then he shook his head and said, "You are a breath of fresh air, Miss Gilchrist."

Again her heart felt buoyed by his words. She

wanted to return his compliment and say something kind about him, but she found she was almost afraid to speak. Would she say too much, something she would regret later? Besides, at the moment the only thing she could think of was, "You are terribly handsome." So she held her tongue and simply gazed up at him.

"I believe the second dance is about to start," he said. "Shall we?"

She placed her hand on his as he formally led her back to the middle of the dance floor.

She had a distinct feeling that she could only compare to how she'd felt her first season, when she was only sixteen and dancing at her first ball—the sudden rush of excitement as the music began to play, knowing that her hair was lovely, that her dress was pretty and fashionable, and that her partner was the handsomest man in the room.

Mr. Watley seemed more relaxed for their second dance, but he was just as attentive. Was he enjoying dancing with her as much as she was enjoying him?

A quite different feeling crept up on her. She always danced with multiple partners at balls. She couldn't even remember the last time she'd danced more than once with the same gentleman, especially two dances in a row. After this dance she must separate herself from Mr. Watley or everyone would say she was just like all the other ladies, in love and vying to be the next Mrs. Watley. And she couldn't bear that. She wasn't like those other ladies.

But Luke Watley's gaze captured hers again until she could think of nothing but how much she enjoyed dancing with him. And about how his shoulders were just broad enough without being too broad. And his jawline was perfectly masculine without being too square. And his clothing was fashionable but without the look of a dandy.

When the dance was over, Jane said, sounding a bit breathless, "I think I shall go find something to drink."

"Allow me to fetch it. Negus? Lemonade?"

"Lemonade, thank you."

As she watched him go, her cheeks heated. Was that from the dance? Or her emotions?

Her thoughts were back and forth, even to the point of scolding herself—first for caring what others might say about her, and then for feeling too much for Mr. Watley.

This was not like her at all. She didn't allow men to addle her like this.

"Are you enjoying yourself?" Penelope was smiling as she gently squeezed her arm.

"I am. But I feel as though every woman is looking daggers at me."

Indeed, when she finally glanced about the room, she saw more than one young lady sending baleful or even angry looks her way.

"You were dancing with a very eligible gentleman. I suppose some ladies will look at you that way. But don't think of them."

"Oh, I won't. I don't care what anyone thinks. I was only dancing with Luke Watley to avoid dancing with Mr. Showalter."

"Sh," Penelope cautioned, a look of alarm on her face.

When Jane turned around, Mr. Watley was stopping behind her with two cups of lemonade.

"Oh, thank you," she gushed, the air rushing out

of her. He hadn't heard what she'd said, had he? She felt sick at the thought. But why should she worry? He'd only danced with her to get away from Miss Trotworthy. He couldn't be offended.

She hadn't danced with him *only* to get away from Mr. Showalter. She danced with him because she wanted to dance with him, because he was kind and gentlemanly and interesting and very handsome. But she couldn't say that.

He handed her one of the cups of lemonade and offered the other to Penelope.

"Oh, thank you!" Penelope said, taking it gratefully. "I was just thinking I wished I had a cup of something, my throat was becoming parched. I'm not used to talking so much." She smiled in amusement at herself before taking a sip. The next moment, she was greeting another guest.

"Penelope is so good. I only wish I could be so good and kind as she is," Jane confessed, studying Mr. Watley's expression for any indication that he had heard the not-so-kind thing she had said about dancing with him only to avoid Mr. Showalter.

"You may not be like Mrs. Gilchrist, but that does not mean you are not kind. Are you kind?"

"I do try to be. I sometimes say things without thinking, though. I am too outspoken to always be kind, and I value my own opinions too much, I think."

Luke Watley looked again as if he might laugh. "You are honest, at least. That is also a refreshing trait, if we are discussing societal rules and norms."

Jane did laugh. "That is very true."

The conversations around them seemed to stop, and Jane noticed more people staring at them. The way she laughed must certainly make her look like a flirt.

She remembered how she had secretly judged the young women who had gathered around Luke Watley at the ball a few days before. She'd seen them as flirtatious and shameless, making their interest in the young widower obvious.

But Jane managed to put the other guests out of her mind.

"How is Jeffrey?"

"He was well when I left him in Hertfordshire two days ago. I am glad he is just a short ride away, but I do miss him when I don't get to see him every day. He has so much energy and spirit. I know the average gentleman never pays much attention to their children when they are as young as Jeffrey, but I find I am not like most gentlemen. I want to know my son, even while he is young."

"I confess, I do not understand the current way of things—ignoring one's own offspring. My mother has always said she disagrees with such indifferent upbringing of children, entrusting them to the care of others. She always spent much of her day with Henry and me, as far back as I can remember."

"And you feel the same?" He was looking at her most intently, even leaning toward her.

"Why, yes. I do. And so does my brother and Penelope."

He seemed to realize he'd been leaning toward her and straightened himself. "It is rare to find a lady who feels this way."

"I believe you are right."

Was Luke Watley thinking of his late wife? She had frequently left her son at their country home in Hertfordshire while she went to London to go to parties and engage in things that could hardly be whispered about. No doubt he didn't want to marry someone like her again.

The dancers were already lined up for the next dance but Luke Watley didn't seem to notice.

"I am curious," he said, his gaze on her as they conversed rather privately against the wall near the entrance to the assembly rooms.

"Yes?"

"How did you end up buying half of the shop from your friend? What made you think of it? Did you always want to own a shop?"

She no longer felt as if Luke Watley was particularly attracted to her. It was as if he was gathering information for an article in the newspaper, so matter of fact was he, his eyes no longer portraying any of the tenderness she thought she'd seen on the dance floor. And that was just as well, since this was more comfortable—talking together as friends instead of flirting.

"I knew my friend Catherine's finances were greatly reduced because of her husband's debts, due mostly to his medical expenses, and I wanted to help her. I had some money that I inherited from my aunt, so I became Catherine's partner. The more I thought about it, the more I liked the idea of going into business, using my money to invest in Catherine's shop. As I started to help her, I realized I could keep the accounts myself, and I actually enjoyed it."

Jane watched Mr. Watley's face. He seemed genuinely interested in what she was saying. The only other time she had tried to explain all this to an eligible young man, he had looked slightly horrified, then his eyes began to wander about the room, as if he wasn't even listening. But Luke's gaze never left her face, and that businesslike, interviewer look was replaced with the same intense expression he'd had on the dance floor.

"I know it is unusual for a woman to go into business, but I am not sorry I did it. And I don't understand why anyone would consider what I did to be scandalous. Why should women not help each other? And if that involves going into business, what could be wrong with that? I don't consider figuring up receipts and expenses to be scandalous."

"No. Indeed not." Mr. Watley looked thoughtful. "I think what you did was a good thing, and there can be nothing scandalous about bookkeeping." He gave the wall behind her an ironic half frown before his gaze returned to her face.

She suddenly wanted to tell him she was sorry his wife had done the scandalous things she had done, had abandoned her husband and child to go to London so often. But of course, she would probably only embarrass him. Besides, it was considered improper to speak of the thing that everyone was thinking or to talk of private and personal matters.

A new group of guests arrived and asked to be introduced to Jane. She pasted on a smile and turned to meet the newcomers, distant relatives of Penelope's with whom she had only just become reacquainted.

Jane greeted them politely, endeavoring to remember their names. And when she turned her head to look for Mr. Watley, he was gone.

She felt a strange sinking in her middle. Was she so disappointed he had moved away to join the party? No, surely not. But she had enjoyed dancing and talking with him, even though the two dances had originally been a ruse to avoid others.

But it was just as well he had moved on. No doubt everyone was saying she was throwing herself at the poor widower, the very thing for which she had silently judged so many other young ladies.

Chapter Seven

Jane danced the next three dances with three different gentlemen. She saw Mr. Watley dance once with Sarah's sister-in-law, but otherwise she scarcely caught a glimpse of him.

The evening went by quickly, with Jane dancing nearly every dance. Henry and Penelope had done well in inviting all the eligible ladies and gentlemen who were in town, it seemed, and she did not see the cluster of young ladies gathered around Luke Watley as she had at the last ball she'd attended. But she began to notice, toward the end of the evening, that he always seemed to be engaged in conversation with other men, moving frequently. Perhaps that was by design.

When the ball was over, the guests bid one another farewell as the ladies' and gentlemen's coats were fetched. As they waited for their carriages to be brought round, they stood idle, talking to Henry, Penelope, and Jane.

While Jane bid farewell to some of the guests, she saw Mr. Watley out of the corner of her eye talking to Henry and Penelope as he prepared to leave. A few moments later, he turned to her and said, "Let me take you home in my carriage."

"Oh, well, I was planning to go with Henry and

Penelope."

"They will be the last to leave, and you look tired. I don't mind taking you."

Did she look tired?

"Go with Mr. Watley, dear," Penelope said, touching her elbow.

Henry said, "He can get you home at least half an hour sooner than we can."

"You did work at the shop most of the day," Penelope added. "You must be tired."

Jane could see what was happening here. She herself had done enough matchmaking to see the signs of their gentle scheming. But if she thought Mr. Watley had any objections to taking her home, she would die rather than allow him to take her.

When she studied his face, she found no aversion in his expression.

"Most of the guests have already gone, if you were wanting to say goodbye to them all," he said, a teasing smile on his lips.

Just then, the servant announced, "Mr. Luke Watley, your carriage is ready."

Mr. Watley held out his arm. "Shall we?"

She placed her hand on his arm. "Thank you." Turning to her brother and sister-in-law, she said, "I shall see you at home."

"Of course." Penelope smiled, but there was no artifice in it. Perhaps her sister-in-law had no ulterior motive in sending her with Mr. Watley.

Jane pretended not to notice the looks from the few guests who were still waiting for their carriages. How she had prided herself on never flirting, especially with the same man with whom every other girl seemed to be infatuated. Now all her efforts to be seen as above the fray had been dashed into the Thames.

Oh well. She had also prided herself on never being afraid of anything, so she wouldn't start being afraid of Society's opinion of her now.

~ ~ ~

Luke noticed it seemed quite dark outside on the street, and he did not see his carriage.

"It looks as if a street lamp is out," he said, as the hair on the back of his neck began to rise. He glanced around but the manservant was nowhere to be seen, and Henry would surely have posted at least one guard.

When a carriage approached, which he knew was not his own, he instinctively moved his body in front of Miss Gilchrist's. Then a manservant appeared out of the shadows, as if he'd been hiding. Another man ran toward them from the other side. Then a hood descended over Luke's head from behind.

He heard Jane's muffled scream as he turned and threw a fist at the man behind him. At the same time, something struck him in the head. A sharp pain radiated down his spine as his vision went dark.

~ ~ ~

Luke awakened to the swaying, jarring motion of a carriage.

"Jane," he said, opening his eyes and trying to sit up. Was she hurt? He had to save her.

The pain in his head had dulled to an ache, but when he raised his head and tried to sit up, his vision began to spin.

Jane was sitting upright on the carriage seat. His head was lying in her lap.

Her hands were on his arms as she gently held him

down. She said nothing. Then he saw the man with the long pistol pointed at them.

"If you try anything, I will kill you both." The man's voice was as sinister as his face, which was illuminated every time they passed a lamppost.

Jane's feet seemed to be braced against the seat in front of them. That and her hands holding onto him must have been the only things keeping him from falling onto the floor of the carriage.

He wanted to show that he was manly enough to defend her from this ruffian and whoever else had snatched them from the street in front of the assembly rooms. But the pain in his head was sharp. He could feel the stickiness of blood on his scalp and in his hair.

"What do you want with us?" Jane sounded quite matter of fact. Many women would probably have been crying at this point, but she behaved as if holding a bleeding man's head in her lap was as normal as playing the pianoforte or going for a walk in Hyde Park.

"You will find out soon enough," the man with the gun said.

Luke waited a few more moments, until he was sure he would not become too dizzy, then he slowly sat up.

The ruffian trained his gun on Luke's upper body. Luke held his hands out so the man could see them.

"You work for Lenoir, do you not?" Luke stared hard, ignoring the pain and slight nausea.

"No more talking," the man said.

Where were they taking them? Besides thinking of Jane and the obvious danger she was in, Luke's mind wandered to Jeffrey. He would be all alone if something happened to Luke, and with the wealth that would be left to him, he'd most likely fall prey to some fortune-seeking distant relative.

In the next moment, as he decided what was most important to him, Luke knew he could not be a coward to save himself. He would save Jane even if it meant he had to give his life to save hers. He could not live with himself otherwise.

But hopefully, if God was merciful, neither of them would have to lose their lives. They both just had to keep their wits about them. *God, please be merciful.*

He noticed the dark stains all over Jane's dress. That was his blood all over her ball gown. Most women would have screamed and fainted over so much blood. But Jane didn't even seem to notice. Instead, she looked cool and collected in the face of a man pointing a gun at her from two feet away.

He would have to rethink all his pre-existing notions about women.

~ ~ ~

Jane steeled herself against all emotion. She had to stay calm and focus her thoughts on how to escape. She could not live with herself if she let something happen to little Jeffrey's only living parent. Jane knew what happened to wealthy, underage orphans with no close relatives, and it was not good.

Luke Watley had lost a lot of blood. It soaked through her skirts to her skin. But she'd applied pressure to it with her handkerchief, which was now completely soaked, and the flow of blood had finally lessened and hopefully stopped. After all, if he lost too much blood, he might be too weak to escape if and when the opportunity presented itself.

Jane was surprised at how angry she felt at being

kidnapped. How dare these men take her against her will, force her into a carriage at the point of a gun, and strike Mr. Watley in the head? It was unthinkable. She wanted to personally give each man responsible a stinging slap and a tongue-lashing that would ring in their ears for days.

But she had to keep her wits about her.

Mr. Watley's hands were tied together at the wrist, but they hadn't bothered to tie Jane's hands. They probably thought her, as a woman, incapable of doing anything to escape. Even unconscious and bleeding, they saw Luke Watley as more of a threat than she was. But she would show them. *God, give me the strength of Samson and the cunning of Jael.*

Jane had always admired Jael for being wily enough to kill a dangerous man and save her people. She was as courageous as any man, and Jane prayed for that same spirit to be inside her now.

She thought of the contents of her tiny purse, which hung from her wrist. There was nothing inside except a few coins and the key to the front door of the town house, even though it was unlikely she would need the key. A servant would be waiting up to let her inside. But she wondered now if she could use that key, which was as long as her hand from her wrist to her fingertip, as a weapon. If Jael could drive a tent peg into a man's temple, perhaps Jane could drive her key into her captor's eye, or his throat. And Henry had told her that if she thrust her knee into a man's groin, he would be incapacitated long enough for her to run away.

She believed she could escape from one captor, and probably even two, but if there were more than two, she wasn't sure if her key and her knee would be weapons enough.

Luke Watley was sitting up quite straight and tall now. He might be able to help her if his hands weren't bound. While there was only one man guarding them, she should try to escape now.

She imagined taking the key from her purse, very slowly and without drawing attention, and leaping at the man sitting on the opposite seat, stabbing him in the throat, and jumping from the moving carriage. But it was speeding through the streets so quickly that she might even be killed by the fall. Besides, she didn't want to leave Luke Watley behind.

She tucked her purse against her stomach, covering it up with her arm. Hopefully they wouldn't notice it and take it from her.

The carriage was slowing, and before it had even come to a halt, the doors were thrown open on both sides. Men reached in and grabbed her and drew a hood over her head, and she managed to clutch tightly to her purse as they lifted her out of the carriage, gripping her arms so tightly each finger was sure to leave a bruise.

Jane thought about struggling, kicking and screaming, but she decided not to. After all, it seemed little could be accomplished by fighting against them now. She was outnumbered and blindfolded.

She felt the damp night air on her skin just before a man's voice said gruffly, "Watch your step." And then she found herself stumbling down some steps, and the sounds of their footsteps echoed in such a way as to tell her she was inside a structure with walls and a ceiling.

When the man leading her stopped, someone snatched the hood from her head.

"Two for the price of one." Lenoir was smirking at them.

"The lady was with him," the man from their carriage ride said.

"You did well to take her. We shall hold them both for ransom. We should get a pretty sum, if this is Henry Gilchrist's sister." He stepped toward Jane. "Are you?"

"I am Jane Gilchrist." Jane was proud of the even, unemotional tone in her voice.

"Why didn't you tie her hands?" Lenoir demanded, glaring at the man who seemed to be the spokesman for the ruffian kidnappers.

"I . . . I didn't think we needed to."

"Tie them." Lenoir threw something at the man.

Jane's stomach sank. How would she fight them with her wrists bound together?

"Let the lady go," Luke Watley said. "She has nothing to do with whatever sordid business you have with me."

There was silence as the man held her wrists together. Jane prayed he wouldn't notice the purse, which she squeezed into the smallest possible ball in her fist.

The man wrapped what looked like dirty rags tied end to end around her wrists and knotted the ends together.

Lenoir looked at her wrists, then moved to Luke Watley.

"You should let the lady go," Luke reiterated.

"Why would I do that? She will bring a good price from her brother."

"And me?" Luke said, snorting derisively. "You won't get much ransom for me."

"You have something I want. Do you know what it is?"

"No, I don't. You ransacked my house. Why could

you not find it?" Anger was creeping into Luke's voice.

"Your wife must have hidden it. She had hiding places, no? Places where she hid important things?"

"I did not see her very much in the months before she died," he said dryly, his lip curling.

Lenoir nodded, crossing his arms over his skinny chest.

How could Anne have possibly chosen Lenoir over Luke Watley? The Frenchman had a certain dark charm about him, perhaps, if one was attracted by that sort of thing, but Luke was much more handsome, and in a completely different way. He had broad shoulders and a powerful chest, light brown hair, and bright, honest, open eyes—or at least he did before the woman he loved betrayed him.

"If you tell me what it is you are looking for, perhaps I can find it for you," Luke added.

"Yes, well, it was something Mrs. Watley had written down on paper, you see. It was a list, possibly in letter form, and she was using it to . . . what is the word in English? Ah, yes. Blackmail. She was blackmailing me."

Luke stood perfectly still. Even his expression didn't change. Finally, he asked, "Blackmailing you for what? What did she want from you?"

"She wanted what every woman wants, no? To rule over the man." He smiled in amusement.

Luke's face reddened. The man was speaking ill of Anne. His jaw flexed but he said nothing.

Lenoir turned to Jane. "I am not a gentleman to say this. That is what you are thinking, no?" He laughed.

"You are a villain, kidnapping and murdering innocent people," Jane said, wishing she could hurt him the way he had hurt Luke.

"Tsk, tsk, tsk." Lenoir made the annoying sound as he shook his head slowly. "You sound very feisty for an English gentlewoman, Jane Gilchrist. But I have never murdered anyone who was innocent."

Jane did her best to slow her breathing and control herself. It would be better if she could pretend to be docile and afraid, but she wasn't sure she was equal to the task.

"It is nearly dawn," Lenoir said. "We will leave you, but when you are ready to tell me where your wife may have hidden the list, you may call out to me. Perhaps I will release you if you give me something useful. Now I must go and write a ransom letter to Mr. Gilchrist."

Lenoir lifted his hand and the other men filed out of the room, two in front of him and two behind him.

So he had four men.

They took the lantern and closed the door behind them, then the sound of a key scraped in the lock, leaving Jane to glance around.

They were in a room, but it was so dark she could see only that they were in a basement room with one small window above their heads. As her eyes adjusted to the light, she saw a mattress on the floor, nothing else.

"Are you all right?" Luke asked. "Forgive me for ruining your dress."

"The dress is nothing, under the circumstances. And I am well. Are you all right? You were bleeding rather profusely."

"I will live. But we have to escape from here."

They could certainly agree on that. But how would they do it? They needed a miracle.

Chapter Eight

Luke tested his bonds, but they were so tight around his wrists that they didn't give at all.

His heart sank again as he thought about how he had inadvertently gotten Jane Gilchrist kidnapped. *God, forgive me.*

Jane didn't deserve this. She might be independent minded, but she was a good woman from a good family and Luke felt sick at the thought that she might suffer because of him.

No, not because of him. Because of Anne. What was she thinking trying to blackmail a man like Lenoir? Was she trying to get money? Or did she have regrets about her involvement with him and trying to free herself from him?

He was always thinking up the best possible excuse for her behavior. Why was he still doing that?

"Are you all right?" Jane asked again.

"Yes, I am well." He had to get them out of this place.

"I will try to get loose," Jane whispered. She started gnawing at the bonds around her wrists, pulling on them with her teeth.

Luke started walking around the small room,

looking for anything that might be used as a weapon. But the room appeared to be completely bare, except for the mattress on the floor. There was not even a blanket.

He tried the door handle but it was locked, of course. He checked all around it, even trying to peek through the keyhole but they must have left the key in the door, for he could see nothing. And the crack underneath the door was not big enough to see much of anything.

He used his fingers to feel around the edges of the bricks in the wall, looking for a loose one.

After perhaps half an hour of this and getting three-quarters of the way around the room, he still hadn't found a loose brick.

"I did it," Jane said suddenly in a low voice, lifting her hands in the air.

She'd gnawed her bonds off with just her teeth. "That's very good," Luke said.

"And I have a key in my purse that we might be able to use for a weapon."

While she was still speaking, Luke felt the mortar crumble around the brick his fingertips were testing. He pulled at it, rocking it up and down and back and forth until it came loose and fell on the floor. He quickly picked it up, holding it against his stomach, since his hands were still tied.

"Let me get your bonds untied," Jane said, taking hold of the brick and placing it on the floor. She began working at the knot.

"It's very tight," she whispered as she stood in front of him. "And are you sure you're all right? You lost a lot of blood."

"I am well."

"You are not even dizzy?"

"No."

"A headache?"

"A slight one. But I am well and ready to fight my way out of here."

"I can fight too. Henry taught me how, and I have my heavy door key and I can stab a man in the throat or the eye. I know how to hurt a man, and I am ready."

"Very good. You don't have to convince me. I won't try to stop you."

"Good."

She continued to work at the knot, and after a few more minutes, she got it loose. His hands were free.

"Your wrists are bloody from the rope." Her voice was strained as she held his hands close to her face.

How soft her hands were. He had missed this. In fact, he wasn't sure Anne had ever touched him with so much care and concern.

"It is nothing." He pulled his hands away from her and picked up the brick. "We need to make a plan."

"Of course. Shall we wait by the door and then attack them when they open it?"

"It might be better to hide our weapons until they come into the room."

"But they will see that our bonds are off," Jane pointed out.

"Perhaps we can make it look like our hands are still tied, drape the bonds over our wrists. And when they draw close to us, we will attack." But this was no rough groom or gardener he was talking to. This was a young lady, Henry's only sister. "No, no, it's no good."

"Why do you say that?"

"We should wait and let them ransom you."

"Why?" She looked at him as if he'd said something

offensive.

"I could never forgive myself if you were injured."

"I won't be injured. I'll stab them in the eye. They won't hurt me."

Luke shook his head. "It is too dangerous. Your brother will pay your ransom and they will deliver you back home, safe and well."

"I can help fight them."

"I cannot allow it in good conscience."

"I am not asking your permission." Jane's voice was slow and even, but there was an edge in her voice.

"Jane—I mean to say, Miss Gilchrist—you must listen to reason."

"Must I? You don't think I can fight. You think I will get hurt. But they may not keep me safe, may not deliver me safely home. These are evil men, and I say we fight. I am not afraid, and the truth of the matter is that you cannot stop me, and I will fight, with or without your help."

Heavens, but she was determined. "Very well, but take my brick. It is a better weapon than the key."

"I disagree. I would much prefer the key, as I have thought a long time about how to use it effectively."

"Very well." But his heart sank even as he said the words. *God, please don't let anything happen to her. If I cannot protect her and she is killed . . .*

He remembered how unbearable the pain had been, realizing Anne had been trampled and run over in the street and he had not been there to protect her, to save her. He wasn't sure he would ever stop thinking about it. Was he destined to feel the same pain and regret over Jane Gilchrist? How would he face her brother if she died? How would he live with the guilt?

He ran a hand over his face, realizing how drained of strength he felt after losing so much blood. But somehow he had to find the strength to fight off their kidnappers.

Jane sat down on the mattress on the floor, which looked dirty in the bare light that was coming through their only window.

He had to admit, she was handling this better than most of the men he knew. But she certainly was not a man, as evidenced by the soft curve of her jawline, her perfect pink lips, the strands of her hair that were coming loose and resting against her cheeks.

"We may as well rest until they come back," Jane said. "Come and lie down. You must surely still have a headache from where they struck you."

"No, I am well. You rest. I will sit by the door and listen for them."

They both picked up their bonds and wrapped them around their wrists without tying them, practicing throwing them off in a hurry and taking up their respective weapons—his brick and her key.

Jane leaned her back against the wall, her wrists draped in the bonds, the key tucked in the palm of her hand. "I don't want to fall asleep," she said, yawning.

"I'll wake you if I hear them coming."

She nodded, closing her eyes and leaning her head back against the wall.

Luke sat near the door, doing the same with the ropes that had formerly been tied around his wrists. Now he just had to listen and wait. And pray nothing went wrong.

~ ~ ~

Jane awoke and quickly remembered where she

was. Her throat was so dry it burned.

She'd tried to stay awake but found herself falling asleep in spite of herself. And since it might be a long time before the men returned, she finally gave in and stretched out on the mattress and fell asleep.

Luke Watley was sitting where he had been before. His eyes were closed but she suspected he was awake. After all, how could anyone sleep with his head straight up like that?

She had dropped her key and it lay on the mattress beside her hand. She snatched it up, adjusting her bonds to make them look like they were still tied around her wrists. Then she stood and looked up at the window.

The sun was out. How long had they been in this room with no water and no food, or any other necessities? Soon she would have to knock on the door and ask to use whatever facilities could be had. She hoped she might be able to at least wash her face and hands, as she felt dirty after lying on the filthy mattress. But more importantly, they both would need some water soon.

Luke Watley was looking at her. How strange to have fallen asleep while he was in the room. But he was a gentleman. He would never do anything untoward.

"How are you feeling?" she asked him.

"I am well. And you?"

"Just thirsty. But I think the sleep did me some good. Were you able to sleep at all?"

"I dozed off a few times. It has been very quiet."

"Do you think they've left us here?"

"I don't know," Luke said, staring thoughtfully at the opposite wall. "If I knew we were alone I could try to break the door down, or at least break off the doorknob. But I don't want to put you in danger."

"Don't worry about me," Jane said. But perhaps *she* should be worried about *him*. After all, their kidnappers might not harm her, being a lady, but they had no qualms about harming him, as they had shown when they struck him unconscious. Her dress, still covered with his blood, was proof.

"I have examined the hinges and the doorknob, and both are quite solid, made of iron. But I might try to knock the doorknob off." He held up the brick in his hand. "But as I said, I don't want to endanger you."

"That is very thoughtful, but—"

He held up his hand, his attention shifting to the door.

Jane heard it too—men's voices coming closer.

Luke Watley stayed where he was on the floor and tucked the brick behind his back, the rope on his wrists looking as it had before she'd untied it.

She made sure her own bonds looked authentic, while the long iron key was covered by her hand.

The sound of a key grated in the lock and the door opened.

A man with a scar on his right cheek came in first, followed by Lenoir. He closed the door behind him and Jane's spirits soared—it was just the two of them.

"I hope you had a good sleep," Lenoir said with a wry smile. "Miss Gilchrist, you will be happy to hear that your brother has quickly agreed to pay ten thousand pounds for your safe return, and he has also agreed to exchange my two men, who were captured in your room, for you and Mr. Watley. So it has been a very lucrative day for me."

His smile broadened and Jane's fingers tightened around her key, which was hidden in her skirts.

She kept Luke in her peripheral vision. As they had agreed earlier, as soon as Luke made a move, she would leap across the four feet between her and Lenoir and strike.

"Afraid your men will spill your secrets?" Luke asked from where he was sitting.

"I don't want to take any chances." Again, Lenoir looked snide. Neither he nor his henchman looked guarded or very alert.

"It's hard to get good help, I'd imagine," Luke said.

"Almost as hard as it is to get a good wife," Lenoir said.

Jane held her breath as she watched for Luke's reaction. Lenoir was baiting him, and she said a quick, wordless prayer that Luke would keep his wits about him.

"That is very true, I'm sure," Luke mumbled, without raising his head or his eyes.

"When will you release me?" Jane asked, trying to sound meek.

"You are not anxious to leave us, are you?" Lenoir asked. "I should think with such accommodations as these, you would wish to stay."

"We need water," Jane said, ignoring his facetiousness and again trying to feign meekness.

"Since you have been such gracious guests, I am sure we can get some water for you. Is there anything else you need?"

Jane shook her head. "No."

"Someone will bring you some water, then."

As soon as the Frenchman lifted his hand, his guard turned to open the door.

Luke leapt to his feet and Jane lurched forward.

Jane thrust the key at Lenoir's throat. His arm flew

up and blocked her. The key struck him lower than she intended and with less force.

She was aware of Luke and the guard tangling behind Lenoir as she brought her knee up as hard as she could between the man's legs.

He grabbed her arms as the breath went out of him. He was falling to the floor, but he brought her down with him.

Jane's shoulder hit the floor first, but she hardly felt it. She struck the man's throat with the key, causing his eyes to go wide and his grip to loosen.

She jumped to her feet and Luke grabbed her hand. "Let's go."

They ran toward the door and she glimpsed the guard lying on the floor. His eyes were closed and blood was seeping from his head.

Luke peeked out the door, then opened it wide and ran. He held her hand so tightly she had no choice but to keep up with him.

They emerged into the sunlight. A carriage was sitting outside the door. The driver glanced down as Luke approached.

"Hey, who are—" the driver began, then let out a yelp as Luke shoved him hard and sent him disappearing on the other side of the carriage.

Luke yanked the door open. "Get in," he said, as he leapt onto the driver's seat.

Jane didn't have to be told twice. She jumped into the carriage as it lurched forward. A moment later, a gunshot rang out.

"God, please don't let Luke get shot," she whispered, remembering how fierce and capable he had looked moments before. She'd never experienced anything before like the power of his presence when he was attacking the guard and leading her away from their kidnappers.

The contrast of his masculinity and strength against his usual gentlemanliness left her breathless in a way she'd never experienced before. Blood pumped through her veins as she realized she hadn't done so badly herself, attacking Lenoir and felling him like a tree.

It was a thrill she'd never imagined she would feel.

She and Luke Watley made a great team. If they didn't get killed.

Chapter Nine

Luke slapped the reins across the horses' shoulders, urging them forward. And then he heard the gun go off behind him.

A quick glance over his shoulder showed a red-faced guard aiming a pistol at them and getting ready to fire again.

He urged the horses to go faster, but the street was too crowded. The horses couldn't go very fast without injuring someone. Luke only hoped the gunfire would alert the authorities, though he knew Lenoir had probably bribed the constable to look the other way.

He just kept the horses moving closer to home and to safety.

Jane had attacked Lenoir quite successfully, leaving him writhing on the floor. And he had managed to put his guard down with the brick with only a bit of a struggle. It had happened so fast, and yet time had seemed to move slowly in those moments. He'd forced himself to feel nothing for the guard, telling himself the man would gladly kill him at a single word from Lenoir.

He and Jane had freed themselves. That was all that mattered. He'd contemplate the possibility that he had killed a man later. Now he had to get Jane to safety.

He drove as quickly as he dared, drawing a raised fist or two and a shouted, "Slow your horses!" from an elderly man who had to jump back onto the sidewalk to get out of the way.

They drew near to where Jane lived. The street was quiet and empty, as it was still a bit early for callers. But it gave him an unsettled feeling to see everything looking at peace, as if nothing out of the ordinary had happened the night before—as if he hadn't prayed all night for God to spare Jane's life as well as his own.

But now he was angry. If Lenoir wanted a fight, Luke would fight him and kill him, if necessary. In fact, he regretted he had not attempted to kill him while he had the chance.

God, forgive me if that's wrong.

He stopped the horses at the front door of the Gilchrist townhouse, jumped down, and helped Jane from the carriage.

Even after being kidnapped and all she had gone through, Jane still looked beautiful. In fact, the unkempt condition of her hair made her even prettier, the natural way it hung by her cheeks—the imperfections making her more endearing, somehow.

But the bloody condition of her dress made him cringe.

He took her by the elbow and hurried her up the steps. Unfortunately, two women had already seen them, stopping short on their walk several feet away, their eyes wide as they covered their mouths with gloved hands.

The door swung wide as soon as they reached it and Henry motioned them inside.

"Thank God you are alive and safe," he said, embracing his sister with one hand and shaking Luke's hand with the other. "What happened? I was just about to pay Jane's ransom."

"We escaped." Jane's voice had an edge of triumph, and there was a small smile lifting the corners of her mouth.

"Oh, my dear!" Mrs. Gilchrist exclaimed as she hurried down the hall and threw her arms around Jane's shoulders. "You are safe! Thank God you are safe!" The usually mild-mannered and quiet woman's voice was choked with emotion.

"It is powerfully good to see you both," Henry said.

"Let us go," Luke said, remaining near the front door while the ladies moved down the hall, undoubtedly to let Jane change out of her soiled dress and freshen up.

Jane stopped and asked, "Where are you going?"

"I will show Henry where we were being held. We might be able to capture Lenoir and his men if we hurry."

Henry was already grabbing his hat from the coat rack by the door.

"I'm coming with you." Jane started toward the same coat rack.

"Absolutely not," Henry said, and with a bit of force.

"You mustn't go," Mrs. Gilchrist said, almost as forcefully.

Jane looked as though she would argue with her brother, but when her sister-in-law spoke, Jane's determined expression softened. Finally Jane folded her arms over her chest. "Very well. But I want to know everything that happens."

Luke and Henry ran to the back to fetch their horses.

They rode as fast as they could, with Luke in the

lead. He remembered exactly which building they had escaped from—a house in Cheapside, not far from the docks. But Lenoir, unfortunately, was not there. Even the guard, whom Luke feared was dead from the head bashing he had inflicted on him, was gone. And though a cursory effort had been made to clean up the blood on the floor, dark red smears could still be seen.

"I shall have this house investigated," Henry said, "searched from top to bottom, and we shall discover who is the owner. I will also post a guard to see if anyone returns to it looking for Lenoir. We shall get him."

They rode back to the Gilchrist townhouse and fatigue set in with a vengeance. Luke's headache returned in full force, his eyelids felt like sand when he blinked, and his whole body ached from lack of sleep.

"Farewell, Mr. Watley. I hope you can get some sleep." Jane went inside the house where her sister-in-law was waiting for her in the doorway.

Still holding his horse's reins, Luke said, "I'm glad we escaped in time, before you released those men."

"I'm afraid the two men have already been released," Henry said.

Luke clenched his fist. If only they'd escaped sooner.

"It is of little consequence, however," Henry said. "Their only importance to us—or to Lenoir—was if they had talked, and since they hadn't yet, it was unlikely that they would. But you did save me ten thousand pounds— Jane's ransom." He raised his brows as if to lift his spirits with that news. "But of course, the most important thing, by far, is that you and my sister are safe. Come and get a drink and some food."

He led Luke into the dining room where he had the

servants bring him a repast. Meanwhile, he scribbled a message and sent it with a servant, no doubt to inform the proper authorities and send men to look for Lenoir and his men.

Luke was just starting to eat and drink when Jane, wearing a clean dress, entered the room with her sister-in-law.

"Do not stop on my account," Jane said, when he stood as she sat across from him at the table. "I do not intend to obey all the rules of polite society with this meal."

The servants brought her a plate and more food, and she began to eat and drink with him, sighing with every bite and drinking as if she were famished. Meanwhile, Henry and Mrs. Gilchrist began telling them how they had experienced the kidnapping.

"My guards had been knocked in the head and dragged out of sight just before the two of you left the assembly rooms to get in the carriage," Henry said. "Apparently the assembly room servants had been bribed to say they saw nothing out of the ordinary. But when your manservant began asking where you were and said you and Jane had not come out when he arrived with the carriage, we began searching for you. A man who was in the building across the street told us he saw a man and woman get attacked and thrown into a carriage by some other men."

"We were so worried and afraid for you," Penelope Gilchrist said.

"We received the ransom letter from Lenoir a few hours ago."

Luke ate a little, but drank more than he ate—tea and a large tankard of ale.

"I know you are anxious to go home, but will you tell us what happened and what you saw before you go?" Henry asked.

"Mr. Watley was very brave and very calm, and we were a great team." Jane smiled straight at him.

Luke's heart lurched in his chest at the look on Jane's face. He smiled in spite of himself, suddenly wondering how interesting life might be if he could spend all his time with Jane Gilchrist.

He cleared his throat to give himself a moment to clear his thoughts.

Then he told of waking up with his head in Jane's lap. Jane filled in the gaps in his story, oftentimes speaking around a mouth full of food.

"Miss Gilchrist was very brave," Luke said more than once in the course of his narrative. "She attacked Lenoir without any hesitation and even though he pulled her down with him, she bested him with only a key for a weapon and left him writhing on the floor."

Jane interjected. "Mr. Watley found a brick, after much searching, and used it to knock the massively large guard unconscious. Then he commandeered the carriage that was waiting out front. With Mr. Watley around, I never really felt as if my life was in danger."

The way she was looking at him made it impossible to look away. Was Jane truly as impressed with him as she seemed to be? Certainly, his wife of three years had never looked at him like that—an expression of both admiration and longing.

Then Jane glanced away, and he wondered if he had only been imagining things.

Both Henry and his wife were quietly watching them.

He had better be careful before assumptions were made about his and Jane's future. As much as Luke had enjoyed dancing with her the evening before, feeling things he hadn't felt in a very long time, he knew he needed more time to sort through why he had been so attracted to Anne, why he had married a woman whose motives others saw through. If he didn't figure that out, he might end up making the same mistake again. And he wasn't sure he could survive, with his sanity intact, a marriage in any way similar to his first one.

"Thank you for your hospitality," Luke said, "but I believe I must go home and get cleaned up."

"You and Jane are a very welcome sight, believe me," Mrs. Gilchrist said, smiling.

As he stood to go, a servant announced, "Mrs. Stapleton and Miss Cuthbert calling on Mrs. Gilchrist and Miss Jane Gilchrist."

"Oh dear," Mrs. Gilchrist said softly, a look of slight agitation on her face.

Jane said, "Penelope doesn't want to say it, but Mrs. Stapleton and Miss Cuthbert are the biggest gossips in London. And this visit proves they saw us arrive half an hour ago." She frowned wryly.

"I should go and reassure them that . . ." Mrs. Gilchrist seemed to be at a loss.

"If you think they care for our wellbeing you are mistaken," Jane said.

"Perhaps we should invite them in," Henry said. "Perhaps we can head off the worst of the gossip before it starts. They may not know anything."

The servant was still waiting. Finally, Mrs. Gilchrist said, "Show them into the sitting room. I shall be there in a moment. Then have tea brought in."

The servant bowed and left.

Gossips. What would this mean? Would Jane's reputation be ruined because she had been out all night with him? Would it even matter to the gossips that they had been kidnapped?

With a sinking feeling, he knew it wouldn't matter, and yes, Jane's reputation would be ruined.

Chapter Ten

"You know I don't care about my reputation," Jane said stoutly, her forehead heating. "Let those gossips say what they will. Any man who is frightened off by them is not worthy to marry me."

Taking tea in the drawing room, sitting opposite Henry and Penelope, Jane had been home from her kidnapping adventure for only one full day and already her brother and sister-in-law were predicting her reputation's demise.

"You know that is not sound reasoning," Henry said, as he and Penelope gazed at her with grave looks of concern.

Penelope added, "A gentleman will not know the truth of the matter, and as a gentleman, he will not ask for an explanation."

"Pish posh," Jane said, clutching her arms, her fingernails making red indentations in her skin.

Henry said, "Luke Watley is meeting with me this afternoon, and I suspect he is coming to speak to me about marrying you."

Jane felt the words physically as the breath went out of her lungs. "Marry me? Why?" But as soon as the words were out of her mouth, she wondered why she had not thought about it sooner.

"Your reputation may not recover from this," Penelope said gently.

"The two of you were alone together all night, Jane. You know what that means."

"But it's preposterous. We were taken against our will, afraid for our lives. There was nothing untoward at all between us. He even had a head injury."

"But it is the noble thing for him to do," Henry said, giving her quite a severe look.

Of course Luke Watley would do the right thing by marrying her. But she didn't want him to marry her only because it was the right thing to do, to save her reputation. She wanted to be married for love's sake, and only for love.

"It is humiliating." Jane felt the angry tears sting her eyes.

"But Mr. Watley is a good man," Penelope said.

"Yes, but I don't want him to marry me out of obligation." Jane could feel her face getting hot, her blood rising. "That is what is humiliating. Can any man love a woman he is forced to marry?"

This was especially hard, considering the unhappy circumstances of Luke's first marriage.

"Of course he can," Penelope said.

At the same time, Henry said, "Yes, of course."

Jane stared back at them, the two of them looking so earnest and—was that hopefulness in their expressions?

"You both *want* me to marry him. Henry has wanted me to marry Luke Watley four years ago, before he married Anne. Well, I won't do it. Let my reputation suffer. It isn't as if a dozen suitors were beating down our door for me before I was kidnapped."

"But Jane." Penelope's eyes were wide.

"You could do a lot worse than Luke Watley." Henry's expression was severe, his brows drawing together.

"But he doesn't want to marry me. He's not in love with me!" Jane's voice was growing quite loud, but she had to make them understand. "I cannot marry someone who doesn't love me."

"How do you know he doesn't love you?" Penelope said.

"I know. A woman knows. He hasn't had enough time to form an attachment to me."

Henry shook his head. "You were always the most stubborn girl."

"Henry." The way Penelope said his name was obviously a rebuke. She scowled at him in her gentle way and shook her head.

"I am stubborn, and you won't see me marrying a man I don't love and who doesn't love me." She regretted her words as soon as she said them, for they could be seen as a criticism of Penelope, who had married her first husband simply because her grandmother had wished it.

Thankfully, neither Penelope nor Henry seemed to catch her veiled allusion to Penelope's lack of love for her first husband and her amenability to marrying someone she didn't love.

"Do you not think you could love Luke Watley? That your feelings will not grow after you are married?"

"That is not my way, to hope that love will grow. It is completely against all my wishes for my husband."

Henry turned away from Jane. "Well, it isn't certain he will make you an offer anyway."

Penelope looked distressed. She opened her mouth to speak, but finally closed it without saying anything.

"I am sorry, but to my own self I must be true, in marriage especially, since it is so important."

"I could understand your attitude if it were anyone else," Henry said, "but the fact is that this is Luke Watley, a good man, a man whose character is above almost any other man you could name."

No one spoke as Henry's words seemed to hang in the air.

"Well, I haven't said I *wouldn't* marry him—if he loved me and if I loved him." Jane crossed her arms and met her brother's eye.

Henry huffed out a breath and strode quickly from the room.

She would never tell Henry or even Penelope, but the first mention of her marrying Luke had sent her heart skipping and soaring. But that made no sense. She was not in love with him, and she absolutely would not marry him unless she was, and unless she knew he was also in love with her. To do otherwise would violate her own inner vows and sense of worth.

As good a man as Luke Watley seemed to be, and as handsome as he was, she was not even tempted to marry him, not without love.

~ ~ ~

After Luke had taken a bath and an hour-long nap, he'd been visited by not one but two of the middle-aged mothers and their eligible young daughters, the ones who had repeatedly called on him ever since less than a week after Anne's death.

He had his servant tell them he wasn't at home, as he simply could not face them, their questions, or their salivating for gossip and reassurance that he was not engaged to Jane Gilchrist, in spite of spending all night with her.

It was a kidnapping situation, for heaven's sake! Surely the gossips would treat this differently. But a third set of callers was announced—this time his neighbor from Hertfordshire, Mrs. Frederick Abbot. Luke bid the servant show her in.

"I came as soon as we heard about your terrible ordeal," Mrs. Abbot said. Her husband was a cheerful man in his late fifties with red cheeks, and her son was an only child and worked in London as a barrister. But neither of them had accompanied Mrs. Abbot.

"How did you hear of it?"

"Mr. Abbot heard when he was at his club this morning. It was said that Miss Jane Gilchrist was also taken, seized right off the sidewalk at the assembly rooms," Mrs. Abbot added, her curls jumping alarmingly to keep pace with her words, her head bobbing up and down as she talked.

"The authorities are investigating it," Luke said, trying to look calm and unconcerned. "You understand that I cannot say anything as to the particulars."

"Of course, of course. But did you give them a ransom? Why did they let you go?" Mrs. Abbot fixed Luke with an intense stare.

"As a matter of fact, we escaped," Luke said.

"Oh, how brave," Mrs. Abbot cried. "And how romantic, to have saved poor Miss Gilchrist. Is she well after her harrowing ordeal?"

Luke cleared his throat. "I wouldn't call it romantic, Mrs. Abbot. But Miss Gilchrist is well, I believe. She was not injured."

"I suppose the two of you are now engaged," Mrs. Abbot went on, lowering her voice, "after spending the night together."

Luke's stomach sank.

He'd had a fleeting thought that this might happen the night before when he was trying to think through all the possible ways he and Jane might escape without being killed. It had seemed too silly, under the circumstances, to worry about such a thing. But now it was happening. These otherwise upstanding women of Society would spread the gossip about him and Jane, and though his reputation would hardly even be tarnished in the eyes of most, Jane's would be forever ruined.

"Mrs. Abbot, you do understand that we were taken against our will, just as we were trying to go home from a ball at the assembly rooms."

Mrs. Abbot leaned forward a bit, as if waiting for him to go on.

"What I mean is, we did nothing amiss. We were seized and locked in a room, but we did nothing wrong." When Mrs. Abbot still seemed to be waiting, he added, "Miss Gilchrist's virtue is completely intact."

"I don't understand." Mrs. Abbot appeared sincerely confused.

"I believe it is I who do not understand you, Mrs. Abbot."

She scrunched her face, as if trying to think how to explain herself, then said, "You and Miss Gilchrist were together all night and now you must marry."

"Because . . . ?"

"Because her reputation is ruined. No other man will marry her."

"So it does not matter that we did nothing wrong.

Her reputation is ruined simply because she and I were in the vicinity of one another during the nighttime hours without the benefit of other people's presence."

Mrs. Abbot again seemed to be waiting, and when Luke did not go on, she smiled and said, "Yes, exactly! Now you understand."

Luke brought his palm up to his forehead and closed his eyes. He let out a long breath.

"Mr. Watley? Are you well?"

He mumbled, "No, as a matter of fact, I was hit in the head, knocked unconscious by kidnappers who could have killed me."

"What is that you say?" Mrs. Abbot asked. "I am rather hard of hearing."

"Nothing. Do forgive me, Mrs. Abbot, but I have several matters of pressing business that I must attend to. You will forgive me if I have my servant show you out."

Luke turned her over to the servant as quickly as possible. As he was hurrying away down the hall, he heard her call out to him, "You haven't answered my question. Mr. Watley?"

He ignored her, quickened his pace, and was soon out of her sight.

This was not how he'd wanted to choose his next wife. In fact, he wasn't even sure he wanted to get married again.

The gentlemanly thing to do, strictly speaking, was to marry Jane. She didn't deserve to have her prospects for the future ruined because she had been at the wrong place at the wrong time—beside him when the kidnappers came, this whole wretched development due entirely to the sins of his first wife.

Jane Gilchrist was so headstrong, and he'd sworn

he would never marry a headstrong girl like Anne. Never again. She had ruined her own life as well as his and cast shame on all connected with her—namely, himself and Jeffrey, her son.

He'd present the matter to Henry. He was a sensible man.

But he was also Jane's older brother and her only protector, since her father was deceased.

Henry was also fair and honest. Besides, Luke would not be able to discuss it with his uncle, the only other person Luke trusted as much as Henry. Uncle Edmund had just gone away to Yorkshire for several weeks on business.

O God, I beg you not to let me make another terrible mistake.

~ ~ ~

Jane went to the shop and gratefully lost herself in figures, adding and subtracting them, sorting and recording them. Numbers were not subject to emotion or arbitrary rules. They were set and certain. They did not change or waver and could not confuse you. They simply were what they were, no more and no less. If one did not like the value or presence of a number, it did not matter. The number was there for a reason, it was solid and steady, and it could not be wished away. And Jane had always found that comforting.

But today, somehow, that usual comfort eluded her. The numbers had gotten into a snarl. The receipts did not match the list of numbers she had recorded, and no matter how many times she added them, they did not come out right.

She looked at the clock. Henry and Luke Watley would be meeting now. Were they discussing her future, deciding whom she would marry? The very idea made her hit her desk with her fisted hand. Well, she wouldn't do anything she didn't want to do. She was a business owner. If Society rejected her as a woman of questionable reputation, why should she care? But she would not be forced to marry someone who didn't love her.

She finally found the mistake in her numbers. She had misplaced a rather large receipt and found it only when she got on her hands and knees under the desk where it had somehow fallen.

"Have I told you how glad I am that you were not killed yesterday?"

Catherine was standing in the doorway of the tiny back office.

"You did tell me, but I'm not averse to hearing it again." Jane let out a pent-up breath and put her face in her hands.

"Well, you don't seem very glad. What's the matter, Jane?"

Catherine had closed up the shop for an hour the day before to call on Jane and assure herself that her business partner and friend was not injured, after hearing the gossip of Jane's kidnapping. But she had been too busy when Jane came in that morning for her to explain about her brother and Penelope thinking Luke Watley would, and should, ask her to marry him to save her reputation. So Jane told her, in as few words as possible, since another customer might enter the shop at any moment.

"Oh my." Catherine put a hand up to her cheek as she stared at the wall behind Jane.

"Yes, exactly. Oh my." Jane had just put herself into a worse mood by talking about it. She chewed her lip, wishing she could yell and scream.

"There certainly are few men more handsome and sought-after than Luke Watley. You could do worse."

"I am aware of that, but I rather wanted a man to marry me for love, and for me to love him as well."

"I see." Catherine was still staring vacantly. After a few more moments, she said, "But you will fall in love with him, don't you think? He seems a good sort of man, and you will be infinitely better than his first wife. He will surely fall in love with you too, after you are married."

"But what if he doesn't? I am not the sort of woman who . . ." How could she explain this? "I will not be satisfied with a marriage that is respectful but distant, without love. I need intensity, Catherine. Am I making sense?"

"Intensity. Yes, 'intense' is a good word for you." She smiled, probably trying to lighten the mood.

"I cannot gamble with my future. I have to know if the man I marry loves me and if I can love and respect him."

"But isn't marriage always something of a gamble? After all, one never knows the person they marry until they are, in fact, married." Catherine suddenly looked sad.

"I'm sorry. It is insensitive of me to speak about marriage when yours ended so recently. Forgive me."

Catherine straightened her shoulders and smiled wistfully. Her voice was softer as she went on. "My husband was quite different after we married than he was before. I believe he deliberately fooled me into thinking he was a better man than he was."

"Because of his gaming debts?"

"Yes, and . . . there were other questionable things. He lied to me more than once. Never trust a man who lies. That is common sense, is it not?" Catherine smiled ruefully.

"I'm so sorry. I thought you were happy."

"I was happy . . . sometimes. But I worried about his character, if I am honest. But I should not be telling you this." Catherine waved her hand and shook her head. "You have enough worries, and all that is over now."

"You know you can confide in me," Jane said. "I would never betray your trust."

"I know. Of your character, I have never had a doubt." Catherine squeezed the hand that Jane held out to her.

"We none of us are perfect, I suppose."

"No, we are not. Why don't you go home, Jane, and see what was said between Mr. Watley and your brother? If I were you, I wouldn't be able to concentrate on the books anyway."

"Perhaps you're right. I am finished with what needed to be done."

After bidding farewell to her friend, Jane found the guard her brother had hired waiting for her. He stoically accompanied her home.

She walked in the front door thinking how she wished she could go to a ball and dance away her frustrations to lively music and good company. And if anyone said one word to her about her reputation after being held by kidnappers all night in Luke Watley's company, she would look them straight in the eye and say, *How dare you accuse me?*

But it was more likely that they wouldn't accuse her to her face. She sighed.

Luke Watley emerged from the drawing room and bumped into her.

"Forgive me—" He stopped short when he saw it was her.

"No harm done," Jane said, starting to walk past him.

"There you are, home early," Henry said, coming out of the drawing room behind Luke.

"I am home early." Jane waited for someone to say something. When Henry and Luke simply looked at each other, she turned and started toward the stairs.

"Miss Gilchrist, if you please," Luke called after her.

She turned, her stomach flipping over itself. "Yes?"

"May I have a word with you?"

"Of course," she mumbled, and led him into the sitting room.

This was the moment she had half expected, half dreaded. *God, give me the words to say.*

Chapter Eleven

Luke followed Jane Gilchrist into the sitting room. He hadn't been this nervous when he asked Anne to marry him. He'd been sure she would say yes, but the outcome of this proposal was much more in doubt.

He cleared his throat, trying to remember what he had decided to say.

As they sat opposite each other, why did his mind choose now to notice how blue Jane's eyes were? And how long her eyelashes were. And how soft her cheek looked.

But her expression was very no-nonsense.

He cleared his throat again.

Jane was still looking at him. He must speak, sooner or later.

"Miss Gilchrist, it has come to my attention that, given the events of the evening of the ball your brother and sister-in-law gave at the assembly rooms, people have begun to say some rather alarming things about the two of us. In situations such as this, with the fact that your reputation is in danger, owing to the kidnapping, which was entirely *not* your fault, I believe I must . . . that is, I wish to ask you to . . . marry me."

Sweat was running down his sides under his arms. He even had to take out his handkerchief and dab at his forehead. And by the amount of heat in his cheeks, he was sure his face was red.

"Mr. Watley, please allow me to put your mind at rest. I do not hold you responsible for what the gossips are saying about us or for the ruination of my reputation. Therefore, I will not accept your proposal of marriage."

She said the words with such a lack of concern, almost with a smile on her face, that he did not know what to say. She was refusing him. He had half expected it, but somehow it still came as a surprise. He didn't know how to reply.

"But, your reputation . . ."

"Mr. Watley, I appreciate your kind concern for my reputation, but I will only marry a man who loves me passionately and with whom I am in love. And since we both know you are marrying me only to save my reputation, then my answer is no."

Luke tried to think what to say. Should he be relieved? He knew he should be. But somehow he wasn't. He wasn't relieved at all.

"Miss Gilchrist, if we are engaged, Society will not ostracize or condemn you. You may not understand what that means, but I have a bit more experience with such things."

"Were you ostracized and condemned?"

"No, but my wife was, and I saw what it would have done to her, had she cared for her own reputation. She was not received by most families of good reputation. Toward the end of her life she was associating only with individuals of ill repute. I do not think you would care for that kind of life, Miss Gilchrist."

Perhaps he had said too much on the subject.

"I am so sorry for all that you have experienced.

Your great kindness to me in this matter is exceptional, and I am grateful to you. But I have my family, my brother and sister-in-law, as well as my mother and a few other relatives, and they will not cast me off. I will not be associating with individuals of ill repute." She looked at him with equal parts compassion and determination. "As I said, I cannot marry anyone who is not madly in love with me, and I do not believe you are madly in love with me."

"I—" He started to speak but was unsure how to reply.

"Are you?"

"No. But that is . . . not the issue."

"It very much is the issue for me, Mr. Watley. And since you surely are not eager to jump into another marriage, and especially where there is no real attachment on either side, I—"

"But Miss Gilchrist, you must realize what a cad I will seem to—that is, as a gentleman, I cannot allow your reputation to be sullied and your position in society to be compromised because of . . ." Because of his first wife, Anne. Because of the mess she got him into, consorting with evil revolutionaries like that Lenoir.

Luke turned away and ran his hand over his face. He tried to pray silently for guidance, but his thoughts were so scattered he could only pray, "God, help me," under his breath.

He should be grateful Jane did not wish to marry him, that she was refusing his proposal. But somehow it reminded him of Anne's many, almost daily rejections.

She hadn't wanted him either.

God, help me stop this manner of thinking. It would not lead anywhere good, he knew from experience.

He'd told himself that Jane was like Anne, but he did not think that was true. Jane would never run around with the likes of Lenoir. It wasn't in her nature. Though she was independent and defiant, she was independent and defiant in good ways, helping her friend whose business, and therefore her livelihood, was in trouble. She was defiant when it came to pandering to Society's hypocrisy. She would not marry for money and power and position. She respected herself too much for that. And that was admirable.

In many ways, she was nothing like Anne.

"I do have an idea," she said, "if you'd like to hear it, that might save my reputation, or at least prevent it from suffering as much as you fear it might."

He turned around to face her, taking a deep breath. "I would very much like to hear it."

"I was thinking, if you agree to it, we could announce that we are engaged. And then, in a few months, we could announce we are no longer engaged to be married, that we have broken our engagement amicably. By then I think most people will have forgotten that there was ever anything untoward or amiss."

"Do you mean, pretend to be engaged?"

"Yes. We will pretend to be engaged, let everyone think we are engaged to be married, then break off the engagement when the gossip about the kidnapping has been forgotten."

Luke took another deep breath and let it out slowly. "It might work."

"I believe it will."

He began to feel more hopeful than he had in a long time. "Yes, perhaps you are right. Everyone will think we are engaged after our ordeal, and when they see that we are the same people as before, that you are the same respectable young lady as you ever were, they will forget about the kidnapping. And when you wish it, we shall say we broke our engagement, and then you may marry any young man you wish."

"And you may marry anyone you wish." Jane smiled.

"Very well. I accept your proposal." Luke held out his hand to her as he would to a gentleman with whom he was making an agreement.

Jane's smile spread over her face as she took his hand and shook it as firmly as any gentleman—though her small, soft hand was not like any man's.

"Let us go and tell my brother and sister-in-law the news—that we are engaged."

"Is it necessary to deceive Henry? Can we not tell them—and only them—the truth of our pretense?"

Jane frowned and placed her finger against her chin in the most charming way. After a few moments she said, "Perhaps that would be best. Very well. We shall tell Henry and Penelope the truth, but no one else."

"They may think it is a bad idea and refuse to help us."

"They won't. You'll see." With the most endearingly mischievous look, she passed from the room ahead of him in search of Mr. and Mrs. Gilchrist.

~ ~ ~

"I am not sure this is a good idea, Jane." Henry gave her a rather severe look after Luke had left.

"You agreed to it."

"I know. I told Watley I would play along, but I do not like it, and I am not sure it will work. I think you should have accepted his proposal of marriage. You are not silly and romantic like other girls, Jane. Why did you not accept him? He is a good man. I can vouch for him. And he is rich and handsome to boot. What more do you want?"

"Silly and romantic? Is that what you call it when a woman wishes to marry for love, not wealth or position?"

"You know what I mean."

"Was Penelope silly and romantic when she agreed to marry you?"

"That is different. Penelope and I were in love when I proposed marriage to her."

"And she wasn't sure you loved her, so she turned you down, did she not?"

"It is more complicated than that." Henry's gaze moved away from Jane's face.

"Every woman wishes to be loved, and I am no different." She was surprised how hard it was to admit that. Just a few days ago, she probably wouldn't have been able to.

Henry was quiet, staring down at the floor. Finally, he said, "I'm sure you are right. Very well. Penelope and I will support you in this charade, but as I told Watley, you and he must make it believable. For all intents and purposes, you are engaged. There should be no suspicions that you are pretending."

"I understand. It would not reflect well on any of us if people discover we were never engaged at all."

"Very true."

"Have you made any progress on finding Lenoir?" Jane asked, changing the subject.

"No, I'm afraid not. It's as if he has vanished. But we will find him. He's probably hiding, afraid, now that we have evidence and witnesses to what he is doing. Now go and get some rest. You both look a bit tired still."

Jane went up to her room to do as Henry said—though not because he said it. She didn't want to admit it, but she'd struggled with falling asleep at night, besides being plagued with dreams when she was able to sleep. Sometimes she dreamed she was in her bed and Lenoir and his guards were coming in her window. Other times she was walking to the shop when men suddenly grabbed her and threw her in a carriage.

Another dream was of Luke Watley lying on the ground, bleeding and unconscious, his late wife alive and well and standing over him.

The dreams had shaken her more than she wanted to admit, but she would overcome this new anxious feeling when she walked down the street, and even when she lay down to sleep at night. Henry planned to install bars over her bedroom window and she was secretly glad.

She was lying in bed reading a book when a knock came at her door.

"These flowers came for you, miss."

The servant presented her with a lovely bouquet of multicolored roses and bright yellow daffodils, two of Jane's favorite flowers.

"Shall I fetch a vase and water?" the maidservant said.

"No, thank you," Jane said. "I shall take them downstairs myself and put them in some water."

After the servant left, she saw the card. It read, *Beauties for a beauty. L. Watley.*

Her heart did a little flutter inside her chest.

Of course, he was only sending flowers because it was a customary gift from a gentleman to his fiancée when they became engaged. But she couldn't help admiring both his taste in flowers and the fact that he called her "a beauty."

Jane felt herself smiling as she carried the armful of flowers back down the stairs.

"They are beautiful, Jane!" Penelope cried as she emerged from her room, and then she gasped. "Are they from Mr. Watley?"

"Yes."

Penelope hurried down the stairs after her. "May I read the note?" She giggled.

"I've never seen you so excited, Penelope." Jane couldn't help but laugh in return. "Of course you may read the note."

Penelope seized the card and read it silently, then sighed. "He is so romantic," she whispered.

Jane wanted to scold her and say it was not romantic when their engagement was feigned and not real, but she couldn't, in case the servants were listening.

Penelope had never been artificial, so Jane feared her sister-in-law truly hoped Luke Watley was in love with her. But Jane knew that he wasn't. He hadn't protested in the least when Jane refused his offer of marriage and gave as her reason the fact that he did not love her.

For several moments, after Jane saw the flowers and read the card, she had the kind of strange sensations that she imagined she would feel if she truly was in love, and engaged to, a man who loved her. And she liked those sensations very much.

Was this deception destined to end badly for her heart?

~ ~ ~

Luke called on Jane the next day, as a good fiancé

naturally would. She seemed to be expecting him, and the flowers he'd sent to her were prominently displayed in the sitting room.

The engagement was beginning to feel real.

Penelope Gilchrist was in the room as well, no doubt for propriety's sake. She had her child with her, who was about a year old, and was playing little games and singing nursery rhymes while she sat on her lap.

"She would make an adorable playmate for Jeffrey, would she not?" Jane was smiling at the little girl.

"She would indeed." Luke felt a fresh ache in his chest at the mention of Jeffrey. "I was hoping to return to Hertfordshire to visit Jeffrey in a few days. Would you like to accompany me?"

He expected Jane to say that she couldn't spare the time away from her shop, or make some other excuse, but she said, "Yes, that will be lovely."

Luke felt an immediate rise in his spirits.

"Would you be willing to accompany us, Mrs. Gilchirst?" Luke couldn't think of anyone he would rather ask to be their chaperone than Henry's wife. "Perhaps Henry will allow you some time away from London."

"As a matter of fact, he has been urging me to go back to our country home and away from such dangers as you and Jane have suffered."

"Yes, do come with us, Penelope," Jane said, her face suddenly quite animated. "It will do us all good to get some fresh air."

"But first, the two of you should be seen publicly together. You can let everyone know you are engaged to be married."

"Is there not a concert or theatrical at which we could promenade ourselves?" Jane glanced around.

"Where is the paper?"

The newspaper was fetched and they soon realized they'd have to settle for purchasing whatever tickets could still be had.

"For myself, I would prefer a theatrical," Jane said, "but if there are no seats remaining, I will be content with a concert. What do you think, Mr. Watley?" She turned her bright blue eyes on him.

"I am content with either. Just don't force me to attend any lectures."

"You dislike lectures?"

"I enjoy learning new things as much as anyone, but I want to learn it by doing it, not listening to someone talk about it."

Jane laughed. "I feel the same about lectures. I once attended a nautical lecture with my father, about how to navigate a ship, and I thought I would run from the room screaming if I had to sit there another minute. I told my father I was ill so he would take me out, but it was not a lie. I did feel ill, but I was instantly better when I could no longer hear the man's monotone voice droning on and on."

Luke couldn't help laughing. "I would have probably done the same, to be honest."

Her smile seemed to turn more intimate, as if the two of them were alone in the room. In truth, Mrs. Gilchrist was so occupied with her daughter that she didn't seem to be paying them any attention.

He couldn't remember the last time he'd laughed.

Tea arrived and he and Jane drank two cups before he said, "I should go and acquire those tickets for the play."

Jane and Mrs. Gilchrist said the usual farewells, but

Jane walked him to the door. She must have been wanting to make sure the servants saw that they were behaving as an engaged couple would.

"I shall see you tomorrow, then," Luke said, his hat in his hand, looking into Jane's eyes.

"Yes." Jane smiled.

Strangely, he suddenly felt a bit nervous, reminding him of his younger self, before he met Anne. Though only a few years had passed, he hadn't thought he would ever feel this way again, the frisson of joyful excitement while gazing into the eyes of a pretty woman.

And not just any pretty woman, but the mysterious and confident Jane Gilchrist.

He bid her a good day, feeling strangely hopeful.

Chapter Twelve

Jane wasn't sure if Luke would return the next morning during visiting hours, but he did, at the same time as the day before, and he brought flowers with him this time.

She happened to be coming down the stairs in view of the front door and entrance hall when he arrived. He held out the bright flowers to her and she took them from his hand. Her fingers brushed his and she felt her stomach do a strange flip. Was she as silly as all that? Perhaps this pretense to being in love was nearly as potent as the real thing.

"I chose the double hyacinths, as they were so intensely blue, they reminded me of your eyes, and the daffodils because the florist said they won't last much longer, as they will be out of season."

"They are very lovely. I thank you. I do enjoy blue and yellow together." As she turned to lead him into the sitting room, she asked, "Is it cold outside?" His cheeks were rather red, but as soon as she asked the question she realized she'd blundered.

"Not cold, only a bit cool," he replied, the color in his cheeks deepening.

Why was he blushing? He spoke quickly, as if he

was nervous. And why did that make her chest feel all warm and buoyant?

The servant who had answered the door came in with a vase of water and Jane started arranging the flowers. "The flowers brighten the room so well. Thank you for bringing them."

"Bringing you flowers is my pleasure."

Mrs. Gilchrist came hurrying into the room, all smiles, and greeted their guest.

"I got your note saying you were able to acquire tickets to the theatrical," Jane said.

"I hope you and Mr. Gilchrist are able to accompany us," Luke said to Penelope.

"Yes, of course. We are looking forward to the play and the company."

They talked of how busy Henry was in trying to coordinate his men in the effort to capture Lenoir and his henchmen. Unfortunately, Lenoir continued to elude them. And then they spoke briefly of their trip to Hertfordshire the next day.

"Henry can only stay one day," Penelope said, "but I shall be there as long as Jane is staying."

Luke asked Jane, "Are you going to the shop today?"

"Yes, for a few hours."

"May I escort you there?"

Penelope looked quite pleased. "Oh yes, that is a good idea," she said, then added, "even though Henry has provided her a guard to accompany her wherever she goes, you can provide her with more interesting company."

Penelope may have meant it was a good idea for him to go with her to the shop so that they could be seen together, to show that they were truly engaged as they were pretending, but this was Penelope. She was happy they would be spending time together only because she wanted them to fall in love.

Penelope had never been the kind of matchmaker Jane was, as Jane had to admit that she had been a bit manipulative when trying to get Henry and Penelope together. But Penelope was obviously not above encouraging a potential match herself.

Jane went upstairs to make some last adjustments —putting on earrings and a dainty necklace—before coming back downstairs to where Luke was waiting for her. When she saw him standing at the door, his eyes locked on hers. That was when her stomach did that flip again. And though it was not unpleasant, she wasn't sure what it meant. Perhaps she should just enjoy it.

She took Luke's arm and they were off to fool the populace into thinking they were in love.

A niggling thought came into her mind, that she might be the one who was being fooled. But that was ridiculous. She and Luke were pretending to be engaged to stop any gossip from flourishing. But when Henry was able to quietly apprehend that evil Lenoir and his men, she and Luke could quietly break their engagement, after six months or so.

At the moment, six months seemed like a long, enjoyable, dangerous time.

~ ~ ~

Jane, Luke, Penelope, Henry, and little Lilith all traveled in one carriage the next morning toward Hertfordshire.

Already Jane had received a few congratulatory notes from her acquaintances on the triumph of landing the season's most eligible gentleman, Mr. Luke Watley.

Never had there been any formal announcement of their engagement, and thankfully, there was no need. Seeing them together at the theatrical, as well as when he'd been seen visiting her, and when they'd taken walks together so many times in such a short period, had convinced everyone that they were engaged. All Jane had to do was gratefully accept their congratulations and well wishes for her future happiness as Mrs. Luke Watley.

This was even easier than Jane had imagined. And she had gone into it thinking it would be a chore and a bother, but it had actually been quite enjoyable. Mr. Watley was excellent company.

Sarah, Lady Ingraham, sent a note saying, "You must tell me how you managed it! The best catch in England, and you refused to even flirt with him. Allow me to add my best wishes for your health and happiness as the new and improved Mrs. Watley. But how many hearts you have broken with this news!"

Jane actually felt a bit sick at the phrase, *new and improved Mrs. Watley*. It seemed too crass even for Sarah.

Jane's reply had been succinct and rather impersonal, both because she was in a rush and because she didn't want to encourage Sarah's cruelty. Besides, it was probably best to distance herself from someone like Sarah, someone clever and cynical enough to discover the truth of the fake engagement.

But Jane would not let herself care about such things now, for she was bound to Hertfordshire, a holiday in the country with some of her favorite people—Henry, Penelope, and little Lilith—and she would get to enjoy watching Lilith and Jeffrey play together as much as she wished.

Luke would be there too, of course. But it was

strange. With each passing day of their pretended engagement she felt more and more unsettled when she thought of him or was around him, at times catching herself feeling as if they truly were engaged.

The last thing she wanted to do was to break the heart of the man who had already experienced more hurt than any twenty-five-year-old gentleman should.

Perhaps she should be worried about her own heart.

No, she would not worry. This was to be a vacation from working—the bookkeeping could wait a fortnight —and from London's smoke and crowds, for the past Sunday was Easter and people were already arriving in droves from the country to enjoy the festivities of the social season.

They all arrived at Luke's country house even sooner than Jane would have arrived at her own home in Hertfordshire, for the Watley estate was several miles closer to London than the Gilchrist estate.

Her first glimpse of Luke Watley's country house was from the window of the carriage. She had seen it before, having been invited to parties and balls over the years, but as she was seeing now in the daylight, Jane realized she'd only ever seen it at night.

She was prepared to give pleasant compliments of it to its owner, but she would not have to exaggerate them.

"It is a most beautiful structure," Jane said. "The color of the brick and the style of architecture contrast well with the white columns." It was also massive, much larger than she'd realized.

"Thank you. It is home," Luke said with an ironic grin.

A thick forest surrounded the house, but not so closely as to shut out the sun, and the house was set on a high point to lend it even more light.

Penelope said, also gazing out the window, "I should think in winter when it snows, that hill in front would be a wonderful place for sledding."

Everyone stared at Penelope.

"What? I am thinking of how much enjoyment little Jeffrey would get from sliding down that hill, and I might even join him. Is that so strange?"

"Not at all," Henry said, smiling. "It's just not what we would expect would be the first thing that would enter your mind." Discreetly, he took her hand and squeezed it, and the look they shared was so intimate and loving, it made Jane's chest ache.

What was she doing, pretending to be engaged to Luke Watley? She should be trying to secure her own happy future, a good marriage to a good man. That was what the Season in London was for, after all. All the balls and parties were for everyone's enjoyment, of course, but also for young unmarried people to make acquaintances and form attachments, with the goal of making a good match.

As they were winding their way up the lane to the house, Luke said, "I am giving a ball—I've already written to my staff to make the arrangements—so that you won't be too bored, Miss Gilchrist."

"I do love a ball, but you needn't worry too much about me getting bored. I enjoy riding and walking as well. I assume you have some good walking trails here?"

"Yes, we have a few." But his brows drew together.

"Perhaps you should not go alone, Jane, as you are wont to do." Henry was giving her his big brother look.

"We haven't captured Lenoir yet, and he isn't likely to give up trying to get what he wants."

"Jeffrey and I can walk with you every day, and I can ride with you when you want to go for a ride," Luke was quick to say. "Or if I'm unavailable, I will have one of my servants accompany you."

"Or you could just give me a pistol to take with me."

"Oh my," Penelope said softly.

Henry snorted. "That won't be necessary. We have servants enough."

Luke at first had opened his mouth to say something, but Henry spoke first. Then her fake fiancé actually smiled, one side of his mouth going up. "I can see you walking through the woods with pistol in hand," Luke said.

"Thank you." Jane smiled back at him, then turned her gaze out the window.

Her heart beat faster, as she couldn't think of a single other gentleman of her acquaintance who would have felt any admiration for her suggesting she defend herself with a pistol instead of taking a servant with her.

"Don't encourage her recklessness," Henry said.

Jane gave him her best disgruntled sister look. "Recklessness." She huffed at him. "It is fortunate for you that I am not a very solitary person by nature. I will surely enjoy the company of Mr. Watley and Jeffrey."

Luke gazed into her eyes. "I want your stay at Dunsmere House to be enjoyable, so please let me know anything that would make your stay more pleasant."

He was the utmost in politeness, but something about his words sent a tingle across her shoulders. Was it his deep voice, coupled with the way he was looking so intently into her eyes? Or was it simply the sincerity of his expression?

"I thank you."

The way his eyes were trained on hers filled her with warmth. It was something intense and intimate, and there was nothing fake about it.

When the carriage stopped, Luke took her hand to help her out. She was not wearing her gloves, wanting to be more comfortable while traveling, as the weather was warmer than usual.

I will not be silly. I will not be silly. But despite her inner vow, the touch of his bare hand on hers caused a catch in her chest. Was she truly so attracted to him? Was she the same as all those girls who had gathered around him at that ball and tried their best to win his attention? And though he didn't say a word, he was giving all his attention to her.

Henry and Penelope were halfway to the door when Jane placed her hand on Luke's arm and let him walk her into the house.

"Welcome, sir," the butler said as he opened the door. Other servants filed out to get their bags and trunks and bring them into the house.

"I would enjoy a tour of the house later," Jane said, addressing Luke.

"It would be my pleasure to give you all a tour, if you wish." Luke glanced at Henry and Penelope.

They both expressed a wish to see the house and settled on an hour from thence, once everyone had rested a bit from the trip.

Jane didn't actually need to rest for an hour, as the trip from London was relatively short. So once she and the maidservant had put away her clothes in the lovely bedroom where she was to stay, she quietly left her room to go downstairs.

In the hall, she heard voices, and one sounded like Luke's, but he was speaking in a low, gentle tone she hadn't heard before.

She started toward the voices, as she got closer, she heard a high-pitched child's voice, crying and talking at the same time.

Jane soon found herself in the doorway of the nursery. Inside, Luke was kneeling beside a child-sized bed.

"What's wrong, Jeffey?" Luke was saying in a soothing voice, leaving out the *r* in his name.

"I don't want you to go," the child said, crying.

"I'm not going. I'm here with you."

"You not here." Jeffrey let out a quiet sob.

"He gets like this after he wakes from his nap," Sally said. "He lets me hold him until the bad feeling wears off."

"You want Papa to hold you?" Luke said softly.

Jeffrey held his hands up and Luke picked him up.

Jane was so close now that she could see the tears clinging to his cheeks as his father held him, rubbing his back. He laid his head on Luke's shoulder.

Just then, Sally caught sight of Jane and Luke spun around.

"Forgive me," Jane said.

"Miss Gilchrist is here," Luke said softly. He turned around so Jeffrey could see her.

"Good afternoon, Jeffrey," Jane said, waving at the little boy by wiggling her fingers at him. "Did you just wake up from a nap?"

"Yes," Jeffrey said, his voice still watery. "Will you play wiff me?" He lifted his head.

"I will play with you."

Jeffrey leaned back and put his hands on Luke's face. "Jeffey play wif you and Miss Gilch'ist."

Jane went into the nursery and sat on the floor. Luke sat in front of her with Jeffrey on his lap, and they played pat-a-cake with Jeffrey until the boy jumped to his feet.

"Jeffey run. You chase," Jeffrey said, jumping out of his father's lap and running out the door.

Jane scrambled to her feet, following Luke as he chased after him.

Luke grabbed his son from behind before he could reach the staircase and swung him up in his arms. Jeffrey squealed.

"We are not to run in the house, remember?" Luke said. "I don't want you to fall down the stairs, so we will go out to the garden."

Jeffrey clapped his hands and bounced up and down in his father's arms, chanting, "Out! Out! Out!" He looked back at Jane. "Come wif!"

"I'm coming!" Jane couldn't help but smile at the little boy's quick mood change.

Once they were out of the house, Luke set the boy down beside the little fish pond. Jeffrey immediately fell to his knees, then lay on his stomach to look at the fish.

"He can be very demanding," Luke said quietly. "You don't have to stay out if you don't wish to."

"Oh no, I don't mind. It is good to be out of doors in the fresh air. When I'm not in London, I like to spend time in the sun whenever possible."

"It is a rather nice day, isn't it?" Luke looked up at the sky. "Hardly a cloud. One seldom sees the sun in London."

"Very seldom."

"Papa, look! Look! I found the Pwince Weegent!" Jeffrey was looking back at them.

Luke squatted beside his son and Jane moved closer.

The pond was only about eight feet in diameter with several brightly colored fish swimming just under the surface.

"Did he say what I think he said?" Jane peered down into the water where Jeffrey was pointing.

"We named one of the fish Prince Regent." Luke grimaced.

"The one with the spot," Jeffrey said, excitement vibrating his voice.

"He is a very fine fish. Have you named any of the others?"

But Jeffrey was too excited to pay attention to her question. He suddenly jumped up and ran around to the other side of the pool.

"Be careful," Luke called, trotting after him. "Remember how much you disliked falling in. You cried and Sally had to give you a bath. Remember?"

Jeffrey simply squealed and pointed at a fish. "That one!"

"It's a blue one, isn't it? What shall we name it?" Jane asked.

"Bluey," Jeffrey said.

"Bluey is a good name. What about that white one with black and orange spots? What should we name it?"

"Spotty."

Luke glanced up and their eyes met. He smiled so wide, with his whole face, that she felt his joy. She had to make an effort to suppress a laugh.

Jeffrey soon grew restless with looking at the fish

and started pulling on Luke's hand and calling, "Miss Gilch'ist, come!"

"I'm coming."

They let the little boy lead them into the trees where he pointed at the ground. "Badger's house."

There was a hole in the ground big enough for a badger to squeeze in and out of.

Before they could warn Jeffrey not to get too close, he held out his little arms and said, "Stay back. Badger mean." He scrunched his face in what he probably thought was a fierce look, curling his fingers like claws.

"They are scary sometimes," Luke said. "We should probably go so we don't disturb the badger."

They all moved away from the hole. Jeffrey went from one thing to the next, calling their attention to a brightly colored mushroom, then a bird feather, and then a broken and empty bird's egg.

After about an hour of exploring, Jeffrey raised his arms to his father and said, "Thirsty."

Luke picked him up, then lifted him up on his shoulders, holding on to his legs while Jeffrey held onto Luke's hair.

"We are very informal here," Luke said, as if apologizing to Jane.

"Info'mal!" Jeffrey shouted.

"I like informality," Jane said, barely holding back a laugh.

They went back to the house with Luke pretending to gallop like a horse, jolting and jostling Jeffrey, with the little boy squealing and shouting, "Go! Giddyap!"

Sally was waiting for them at the back door and took Jeffrey to the kitchen for something to eat and drink.

"I believe we are late for tea," Luke said, his brows

raised in apology. He made his way through the hall toward the indistinct voices somewhere ahead. "Forgive me, Miss Gilchrist. You will think me a very bad host."

"Not at all. I am enjoying myself immensely."

They entered a large sitting room where Henry and Penelope were already having tea.

"Forgive us for starting without you," Penelope said, "but the servant said you were exploring the garden with Jeffrey and we didn't know when you'd return."

"Forgive me for being late," Luke said.

Penelope poured them both a cup of tea, which was still warm, and they ate biscuits and talked of what they'd seen and done with Jeffrey.

"I can hardly wait until Lilith is old enough to walk and explore out of doors," Penelope said.

Jane had very much enjoyed her time with Jeffrey and Luke. She felt as if there was a new familiarity between them. When she caught Luke looking at her, there was the same frisson, but with less nervousness. But that was normal, she supposed, for two people who were pretending to be engaged.

Chapter Thirteen

The next day Luke was glad the weather was still holding out, as it had been cooler and wetter ever since the New Year had begun.

And once again Jane just happened to be around when Jeffrey was awake and wanting attention from Luke.

The day progressed much as it had the day before. Luke watched as Jeffrey began to sidle up to Jane more often, even seeking her help when he dropped his toy animal and it went under a table. And when he became out of sorts, crying over a little fall, then rubbing his eyes, she held out her arms to him and he climbed into her lap.

"My mother used to sing this song to me." Jane looked into Jeffrey's eyes and started to sing a lullaby that Luke vaguely remembered his nurse singing to him.

Jeffrey stared at Jane's lips as if mesmerized. His head started drifting closer to her chest, but then he pulled himself straight and rubbed his eyes again. But after another instance of that, he finally succumbed to her soothing voice and the slow, gentle words of her song, and lay his head against her and closed his eyes.

Jane wrapped her arms around him, very lightly and gingerly.

Luke's heart seemed squeezed by a giant fist inside his chest. Was this the independent Jane, who cared nothing for convention and other people's opinions, whom he'd compared to Anne as someone similar? Her face was angelic as she sang and tenderly held his son in her lap. His heart clenched again.

As Jane continued to sing, Jeffrey sank deeper, until he was completely relaxed and would sleep through almost anything, from Luke's prior experience.

"I'll go get Sally to put him to bed."

"I can take him to his bed," Jane whispered. She stood up, cradling Jeffrey in her arms.

Luke led her to the nursery, where Jane laid him down and covered him with the sheet.

Sally walked into the room and whispered, "I'll watch him now."

Jeffrey and Jane left the room and he closed the door.

"Thank you for letting me do that," Jane said. "I enjoy when Lilith lets me sing her to sleep, but she rarely ever does. She always wants Penelope when she's sleepy."

Luke didn't trust himself to speak as he gazed down at her. Could she be real? A woman who was confident in her ability to run a clothing shop in London and do the bookkeeping, while also enjoying what most women would leave to their child's nurse—comforting and holding their child while they fell asleep? Most ladies of Society considered such care of children, even their own, to be beneath them.

Jane was indeed an unusual woman.

He'd always thought, since the many problems in his first marriage, that he wished to marry someone like Penelope, who was sweet and soft-spoken, conventional and sensible. But Jane was definitely not soft-spoken or conventional, which only seemed to attract him more.

What if he made another terrible mistake?

But their engagement was not real. He had nothing to worry about, as long as he didn't actually marry her.

The other problem was that the more time he spent with her, the more he thought about marrying her. Fortunately, his fears, especially the fear that Jane might reject him and break his heart the way Anne had, would keep him from doing anything impulsive.

A new problem had begun to dawn on him. What if Jeffrey became attached to Jane? When they broke off their engagement and stopped spending time together, Jeffrey would be brokenhearted when she suddenly disappeared from his life.

What had he gotten himself, and his son, into?

~ ~ ~

Jane was careful to avoid Luke and Jeffrey the next day.

It had been a mistake, she realized, to sing Jeffrey to sleep. The feel of the little boy in her arms, knowing he had no mother, having already spent so much time with him, had created some pretty intense feelings inside her. And though she would be fine, she didn't want to hurt Jeffrey by letting him get attached to her. In a few months she and his father would no longer be engaged, even in pretense, and Jeffrey would suddenly cease to see her.

But perhaps she was overthinking.

Jane took her morning walk with one of the groomsmen. She went early, while everyone else would still be at breakfast. The woods that had seemed so full of wonders and so interesting the day before seemed rather drab and dull today. She thought of Jeffrey's happy little voice at every turn, as well as of Luke's kindhearted way of encouraging his son's curiosity and independence.

Luke's gentle manner with his son, the way he was so attentive and kind and affectionate, was working on Jane in ways she'd never imagined. What could she possibly want with the average gentleman, who would ignore his son until he was at least twelve years old and could go shooting with him? A man who was quiet and aloof would never interest her again. A man who was arrogant and self-important and couldn't be bothered with being kind and patient was so completely unattractive to her, especially now, after seeing Luke with his son.

Those other ladies who had fawned all over him had never had the opportunity to see Luke with Jeffrey. They would probably faint with love for him if they did.

But perhaps other women did not realize, as Jane had not fully realized until now, that a man who was patient and kind—while remaining masculine and confident in himself—was infinitely preferable. Many young ladies were silly about such things as fashionable clothing and perfect hair and the way a man sat on his horse. But those things did not matter at all in a husband.

Jane stayed in her room, writing letters she owed to relatives and friends, for the part of the day that she imagined Luke would be playing with Jeffrey. She would not be drawn in by the handsome father and son. She would not be like those ladies who fawned over him at balls.

Thinking of balls, she remembered that Luke's ball would take place in three days. She'd better prepare herself to pretend to be engaged to him, which meant dancing mostly with him all night.

That evening at dinner, Penelope said, "Jane, I hardly saw you all day. Are you well?"

Luke looked up, obviously listening.

"I am very well," Jane said. "I had a lot of letters I had been putting off writing. I am caught up now. And I took an early morning walk while the air was still very cool."

Luke was quiet, staring down at his soup.

"But I would love some company tomorrow. Perhaps we could all go on a walk and have a picnic. Is there a good spot somewhere for such a thing?" Jane directed her question at Luke. At least if they were all together in a large group she would be able to keep a bit more distance between them—both emotional and physical.

After dinner, when they moved into the drawing room, Penelope was persuaded to play and sing. When she was done, they all thanked her for gracing them with her talent.

"Have you thought of a good place for our picnic?" Jane asked their host.

"I believe I do know just the place," Luke said, becoming a bit more animated. "It's not far from the house, near enough that the children can join us for a while, and then their nurses can take them back to the house for a nap."

"That is very thoughtful," Penelope said.

"There is a stream nearby that is pleasant to listen to, and also shallow enough that the children can play in the water and not get hurt. And there is a nice shady area near the stream so we won't have to worry about the ladies getting too much sun."

"You have thought of everything," Penelope said.

Jane was thinking the same thing.

"I spoke to the housekeeper and we can go for our picnic tomorrow at one."

"Will they be able to get everything ready so soon?" Penelope asked.

"Since there are only a few of us, it will not be a problem. So we are all set, unless the weather turns foul."

The next morning was bright and clear but rather cold for a spring day.

Jane walked with Penelope and Luke, the two children just ahead of them, being carried by their nurses. The servants had already gone to set up the food and to prepare a place for them to sit.

Jane asked Penelope, "I wonder how Lilith will react to the little stream Mr. Watley spoke of. Will you let her play in the water?"

"Since it is rather cold today, I think it best not to let her get very wet, but we will see if she wants to put her hands in the water."

"And Jeffrey?" She smiled, turning to Luke. "Will you let him play in the water? I'm eager to see his reaction. Has he played in the stream before?"

Luke's expression was unusually severe. Could her questions have displeased him?

"We shall see," he said. "It is rather cold."

And so was his answer and demeanor.

They weren't actually engaged, so he didn't have to be anything more than civil. She couldn't help wondering, however, if something was bothering him.

The walk to the picnic spot was much shorter than the walk Jane normally took, so she said, "I shall walk a bit further. Does anyone want to join me?"

"Take one of the servants with you," Luke said. He

got the attention of one of the footmen who had carried the food baskets and said, "Go with her," without even looking at Jane.

He might have offered to accompany her. But again, he was under no obligation to take a walk with her. Perhaps he just wanted to spend time with Jeffrey. Still, it put her in mind to be less open with him.

As she walked deeper into the forest, she noticed that the trees were finally growing new leaves. A few wildflowers were blooming too, waking from their long winter sleep.

Jane was just about to turn around when she thought she heard something. She stopped and looked behind her, and the footman did as well.

The sun, which had been so bright earlier, was now hidden behind the clouds, making the woods look much darker. She searched the shaded places between the trees but saw nothing unusual and nothing moving.

"I thought I heard something," Jane said.

"Shall I go look?" the footman said.

"No, it was probably only a bird or a badger. I am ready to go back now."

"Very good, miss." The footman walked just behind and beside her, letting her take the lead. She moved over to walk in the clearing instead of among the trees and kept looking over at the dark wood. It was not sensible to think she could feel someone's eyes on her, and yet that was precisely how she felt.

She glanced over at the footman but he seemed oblivious.

Quickening her pace, she continued to check the tree line, but she never saw anything. When she arrived back at the picnic area, Luke and Penelope were laughing and watching Jeffrey and Lilith sitting on a blanket opposite each other. Lilith was also giggling as Jeffrey tried to play pat-a-cake with her.

"There you are," Penelope said. "Shall we eat?"

"Forgive me for causing you to wait for me."

"No, no, we were letting the children play. All is well. Come and sit." Penelope patted the blanket and Jane sat between Penelope and Luke. The servants helped pass the food out and Luke and Penelope placed everything on the blanket in the middle, with the nurses helping to feed the children and keep them occupied while the adults ate.

Jane noticed Penelope drawing her woolen shawl tighter around her neck.

"It is colder than I anticipated when I suggested this picnic," Jane said, wincing. "It is all right if you want to go back early."

"It is rather cold," Penelope said, "but we can take a walk to warm ourselves."

"I think Jane is right. We should not stay out too long." Luke was looking at Jeffrey, whose nose and cheeks were already turning red from the crisp air.

Since the picnic had been Jane's idea, she felt a bit deflated that it was not going as she'd hoped. But Luke needn't be so grumpy simply because the weather was cold. The children were adequately bundled in warm clothing, including woolen hats.

They ate the food in silence that was broken only by the children's grunts and squeals and whines. Soon Lilith became quite fussy.

"I don't think we should try to play in the w-a-t-e-r today," Luke said, spelling out the word in case Jeffrey was listening.

Jane said nothing. After they had eaten, the wind

grew stronger, sending a chill across her shoulders. As it began to look quite stormy, Luke instructed the servants to pack up the picnic baskets and they all stood to their feet to walk back to the house.

Jeffrey asked to walk with Luke, and by the time they arrived, he was falling asleep on his father's shoulder. Lilith was also ready for her nap, and suddenly Jane found herself alone.

She wandered into a library or reading room on the ground floor, filled with bookshelves and cozy armchairs, and she went to choose a book from the shelves lining the walls. She was still searching a few minutes later when she heard someone come in.

Her eyes met Luke's at the same moment and he stopped short.

"Forgive me. I didn't know anyone was here," he said, starting to turn around.

"You needn't leave on my account," Jane said, noticing the sour tone of her voice, which she had failed to suppress.

"I don't wish to disturb you."

"You will not disturb me, as I'm just looking at your books, and you might as well retrieve whatever it was you came here for."

"Very well." He went to the shelf and in a few moments found a book and tucked it under his arm.

"Forgive me for saying so," Jane said, "but you seemed a bit out of sorts at the picnic. Was it only the weather? It has been quite cold and wet this spring."

Luke stared at the floor a moment, then said, "Truthfully, I wanted to tell you that I think it best you not interact too much with Jeffrey. I don't wish for him to become attached to you, only to have you disappear from his life when our charade is over." The words, *as his mother did*, seemed to hang in the air.

"I see." And Jane did see. She understood what he meant, and she didn't even disagree with him. But it stung, an actual physical pain in her chest that took her breath away and made her cheeks burn, to have him warning her away from his son. "I suppose it was a bit much to sing him to sleep and put him to bed yesterday."

"It is only because we are not engaged. I simply don't want my son to be hurt. Again. It is not meant as a criticism of you. I—"

"Of course. No. I understand."

"Forgive me if I sound rude."

"No, you are right, quite right, I am sure." But she could not meet his eye anymore and was relieved when he started toward the door.

"I shall see you at dinner," he said, and practically ran from the room.

Jane's stomach roiled and her face remained hot with embarrassment. She would never hurt Luke's precious, handsome, sweet little boy for anything, but it seems she might already be destined to hurt him, if indeed he had formed an attachment to her.

She thought hard about the picnic. The child had smiled and waved to her when he saw her, but he had been much occupied—and fascinated—with Jane's little niece Lilith. Sally and Luke had hovered around him as well. Was that by design, to keep him away from Jane?

No doubt, Luke was thinking she should never have held Jeffrey and sung him to sleep. But she refused to feel ashamed for doing so. And how dare Luke judge her so harshly simply for being kind and affectionate to his son? Furthermore, she assumed this meant that Luke had absolutely no intention of ever marrying Jane.

Well, if he felt nothing for her, she certainly wouldn't allow herself to feel anything for him. But it was too late for that, apparently. To think he didn't even entertain the possibility that they might marry someday hurt so much it took her breath away.

And somehow, even though she and Penelope were staying at his home for several more days, including a ball during which she was supposed to pretend to be engaged, she had to avoid all contact with Jeffrey.

Jane left the bookshelves and slipped outside to the garden.

The cold air felt good on her face. But she wasn't sure she'd ever been so out of sorts. She was angry and embarrassed and unsure how she should feel. Before this moment, no one had ever told her to stay away from anyone, especially a young child.

She stayed close to the house, not paying attention to the rose bushes or hedges or the little fish pond, as her thoughts kept her distracted. But then she saw a man at the other end of the garden, watching her.

Jane stopped and stared at him, and he slipped into the cover of the trees and disappeared.

She wasn't supposed to be out of doors alone. But at the moment she felt as if she could fight off two kidnappers at least, with the blood surging through her veins and making her clench her hands into fists.

She stared at the place where she'd seen the man, but there was no other movement, so she went inside.

Telling Luke that she'd seen a man at the edge of the garden seemed like the prudent thing to do, but she felt like she could not face him—not now, and possibly not ever again.

Yet, Jane Gilchrist was no coward. She would see Luke again at dinner and would not hide in her room like someone who had something to be ashamed of.

The man she'd seen was probably the gardener and nothing to be alarmed about.

Chapter Fourteen

Luke could see that his words either embarrassed or angered Jane—probably both—but Jeffrey was his son, and he had to protect him. His son had already lost his mother, though truthfully, Jeffrey hadn't asked for her in months.

When Luke put Jeffrey to bed the night before, he'd looked up at Luke with those big, innocent eyes and said, "Where Miss Gilch'ist? I want Miss Gilch'ist sing."

"I can sing to you. What do you want me to sing?"

"No. Miss Gilch'ist sing."

"Sally will sing you a lullaby."

The nurse, who was laying out the child's clothes for the next day, came over and started singing.

"No!" Jeffrey said peevishly. "I want Miss Gilch'ist." He started crying and rubbing his face, obviously tired. It took several more minutes to settle him down, with him refusing to let either of them hold him. Finally, he fell asleep with a tear clinging to his cheek.

Luke knew then that he had to protect his son from getting even more attached to Jane. She would be out of their lives in a few months.

If he was honest, it might be his own heart he was trying to protect. When he'd watched Jane holding his son, singing so softly and sweetly to him, it had broken something inside him, opening a hole in the wall he'd built to protect himself.

As he lay in bed that night, he felt a yearning, stronger than anything he'd felt since he'd married Anne, something he never imagined he'd feel so soon after her death. He found himself imagining what it would be like if he had married Jane instead of Anne, and what it would be like if he was married to Jane now.

Besides the fact that such thoughts seemed wrong, he knew he couldn't marry again. He couldn't allow himself to be in love again. It was too painful. And it was his responsibility to protect both himself and Jeffrey.

To Jane this pretend engagement might be a fun game, like chess or cards, but for him, there was too much at stake.

He couldn't bear to lose again.

~ ~ ~

Jane avoided Luke and Jeffrey for the rest of the day, but she went to dinner and looked Luke in the eye, refusing to let him make her feel as if she'd done something wrong.

An air of tension hung over the dinner table, and poor Penelope, not knowing what was amiss, tried to carry the conversation by herself, even though she normally preferred to let others do most of the talking.

Jane did her best to behave as if nothing had changed. But when Luke went to bed immediately after dinner instead of sitting with her and Penelope in the drawing room, she knew he was avoiding her too.

When she and Penelope were alone, Penelope asked, "Did something happen between you and Luke? You seemed to be getting along very well, but tonight I sensed something was wrong."

Jane couldn't lie to Penelope, and she ended up telling her what Luke had said.

"I am sure he is only worried about Jeffrey. It shows that he is afraid . . ." Penelope stopped and pursed her lips.

"Afraid of what?"

"That he might fall in love with you, but you won't fall in love with him."

"Penelope, only you could think such a thing, in all your optimism. Obviously, Luke just doesn't care for me and wants me to stay away from his son."

"I disagree. You don't know what it's like to have a spouse break your heart over and over, Jane. It creates a fear inside you, fear of letting that happen again. I was so afraid that I refused Henry's first proposal of marriage."

"I know I don't know what that is like, but in my opinion, his warning me away from his son shows that he has no intention of ever marrying me." Jane folded her arms over her chest, something for which her mother always scolded her. But she was in no mood to care about looking ladylike.

"You should speak to him about it and tell him that whether you marry or not, you will not disappear from Jeffrey's life as long as Jeffrey wishes to see you. If Luke knows you are committed to seeing Jeffrey—once every two weeks, for instance—then he might stop worrying about him."

"I have no desire to speak with him about it," Jane said. "I did nothing wrong and he has made it seem as if I was careless and insensitive, as if I tried to hurt Jeffrey, and I would never do that."

"That is the very thing you should tell him."

"No." How could she? She would not crawl to Luke

Watley and beg his permission to interact with his son. "Jeffrey is Luke's son, and if he wishes me to keep my distance, then I shall keep my distance."

Penelope sighed. "I understand, but . . ." She said nothing for a few moments, then went on. "The ball is tomorrow night and you and Luke will have to pretend that you are happily engaged. Will you be able to do that?"

"I can do it if he can."

"If you remember, he proposed marriage to you. He would have married you, but you refused him."

"If *you* remember, he only proposed marriage to me to satisfy the gossips."

"I am not saying you should have accepted him. I am only saying that you cannot accuse him of not wanting to marry you."

"Perhaps he was willing, but he obviously doesn't want to marry me now."

"Jane." Penelope's voice was gentle, the look in her eyes so earnest.

"What?"

"If you've changed your mind . . . if you wish to marry Luke Watley . . ."

"What makes you say that?"

"If you do, then you should let him know how you feel."

"So he can tell me he wants nothing to do with me? No thank you. I will not be like those young ladies who gather around him at parties and balls and fawn over him, leaving him in no doubt that they would marry him at a moment's notice."

Penelope looked back at her, her normal, placid expression returning. "Perhaps pride is not your best friend in this situation."

Jane's breath rushed out of her, sounding like an exasperated sigh. "If I were in love with him, perhaps I would behave differently, although I don't think so. I have never been one to throw myself at a man, Penelope. It is not my way. And I have not known Mr. Watley long enough to know if I might fall in love with him. I expect to marry a man of utmost integrity who is madly in love with me and I with him. Why should I settle for less than that? And does that make me prideful?"

Penelope's mouth went up at the corners in a tiny smile. "I don't believe you should settle for a man who doesn't love you. As for pride, I do not wish to judge you, only to put you on your guard against such a thing. You know I love you as my own sister."

"Forgive me," Jane said rather grudgingly. "I get too passionate sometimes, and I know you are the sweetest sister I could ever have, but . . . to be honest, I was quite stung by Mr. Watley's words about staying away from Jeffrey." All the vinegar had left her suddenly, and she was left with only the pain of Luke's rebuff, a heavy feeling in her chest.

Penelope placed a gentle hand on Jane's arm and made a sympathetic sound in her throat. "I'm so sorry. It does seem a bit harsh."

"I do understand, I suppose." Jane sighed. "But now he has made everything awkward between us, and I must face him tomorrow night at the ball in front of so many people." Jane placed her hands over her face and made a growly noise.

"Do not worry. You are pretending to be engaged, so pretend you are not feeling awkward."

Penelope's smile had grown quite big. Jane knew she and Henry would be amused by Jane's predicament.

But she deserved to be laughed at, Jane supposed, since she had been the one to suggest they pretend to be engaged.

Evil Lenoir. Why couldn't he have kidnapped some other woman with Luke?

But that thought—imagining Luke asking another woman to marry him to save her reputation—made the heat rise up inside her, just before her stomach felt sick.

She did feel some attachment to Luke Watley. Perhaps more than she was willing to admit. It was all so demoralizing.

~ ~ ~

The housekeeper came to Jane and said, "Mr. Watley says if you'd like to make the decisions about the ball tonight—the refreshments and decorations—he'd be much obliged. But if you'd rather not . . ."

"Thank you. I don't mind." Jane went with the housekeeper and made the decisions, though there was little to decide. The household had managed balls before, though not very many, and Jane simply had to select the refreshments to be provided, as well as choose from a small list of decorative foods and decor to use as centerpieces for the tables.

Jane was getting a taste of what it would be like to run a household, as a wife would be expected to do. And she found she rather liked it. She was not one to doubt her own decisions, as Penelope sometimes did, and she enjoyed having the kind of control the mistress of Dunsmere House would have, free to entertain her guests as she preferred. And since Luke's servants, especially the butler and housekeeper, were competent, there were no onerous tasks, such as correcting shoddy work, laziness, or frequent mistakes.

Of course, she was pretending to the servants, as she would be tonight at the ball to the guests, that she was in love and engaged to be married. But she had only to remember that Luke had told her to stay away from Jeffrey to remind herself that not only was she not engaged to Luke, she never would be.

The day was rather cold and started off with a light rain, but that would not deter the guests, she was sure. They were too eager to see the couple who had been kidnapped and then became engaged immediately after. No doubt they wanted to see for themselves if Luke and Jane were in love, or if they got engaged just to save their reputations.

"You have such a cynical attitude about people sometimes," her mother had said, half scolding, a few years before.

Jane didn't necessarily want to be cynical, but she also would rather be cynical than foolishly trusting people who didn't deserve her trust.

Her mother had also once called her "intrepid," and she did rather like that label. She had no intention of letting herself be intimidated by this situation—guests who were passing judgment on their engagement, and a fake fiancé who wanted her to stay away from his son.

She had to admit, she was still angry and a bit embarrassed by that. And she wasn't sure how she would pretend to be in love with Luke.

Jane dressed very carefully, the way she imagined a woman in love would, allowing the maidservant to style her hair with a few extra curls, as well as ribbons and pearls. She wore her most feminine gown, a pale pink satin decorated with lace and flounces. It was nothing out of the common way, but Penelope had once told her that the color brought out "the perfection of your skin."

Jane didn't think her skin was perfect, but the color was rather becoming, if she did think so herself, in contrast to her dark brown hair and unfashionably tanned skin.

She went downstairs early to look in on the servants and the preparations for the ball. When she turned a corner, her face smacked into Luke's chest before she could stop herself.

"Miss Gilchrist! Forgive me." Luke held on to her upper arms as he stepped away from her.

Her own hands were pressed against his chest to steady herself. "I didn't see you."

"Forgive me. I wasn't watching where I was going." He looked quite distracted, but then his eyes roamed from her hair to her dress before snapping back to her face. His throat bobbed as he swallowed. "You look very . . . pretty. That is, you look lovely."

"I thank you." She gazed into his eyes, marveling again at the depth of emotion she found in them—until she remembered that she was angry with him.

"You seem as if you are in a hurry," she said, dropping her hands from his chest.

He suddenly let go of her arms, then cleared his throat. "Yes. The grooms saw a man lurking about. I was on my way to see if I could catch sight of him."

"Don't let me slow you down." Jane stepped aside to let him pass.

"Thank you. Forgive me," he said again, then hurried past her toward the back door.

Jane suddenly realized what he'd said. She should tell him that she'd also seen a strange man out by the garden.

She hurried after him.

~ ~ ~

Luke turned around and saw Jane. Surely she wasn't following him.

He continued toward the trees next to the stable where the grooms had seen the strange man. The fact that Jane was just behind him made him wish he had retrieved a gun before going out. But he continued on, not wanting the man to get away. As long as he kept his body between her and the man, she should be all right, and the grooms were all standing outside the stable and would come to help if they needed them.

He went to the tree line as one of the grooms joined him. They saw nothing, and he didn't want to go too far, as he was already risking his clothing and didn't want to change again before the ball.

He blew out a breath. "I suppose he's long gone."

"Yes, sir. But we'll keep an eye out for the blighter."

"Good man. Keep me informed, and pin him down, if you can."

"Yes, sir."

When he came out of the woods he saw Jane. She'd stopped just short of going into the trees and was holding up her skirts an inch or two.

Luke had little experience of women, since his mother died when he was young and he had no sisters. And he almost felt he hadn't had enough time with Anne to give him a healthy glimpse into the thoughts and needs of a woman, but it seemed wise not to mention that she was in danger of spoiling her dress.

"Did you find him?" she called.

"No." It was tempting to tell her that there was no need for her to follow after him when he was searching for a possibly dangerous man.

"I saw a man in the garden yesterday."

"What do you mean?"

"There was a man at the edge of the garden, near the tree line. But when he saw me, he moved into the trees."

"Why didn't you tell me?"

She bristled at his question, folding her arms across her middle, her brows lowering. "I thought he might be the gardener."

"Were you outside in the garden alone?" His tone was more accusatory than he'd meant for it to sound.

She glared back at him. "You may not order me about, as I am not your wife, nor am I ever likely to be."

She mumbled the last several words, but he heard them.

So she was offended by his requesting her to not let Jeffrey become attached to her. It was obvious. And Jane's defiance was quite familiar. Hadn't Anne spoken to him in just such a way when he'd begged her not to go to London by herself? She'd let him know, in no uncertain terms, that she was not his servant nor his slave and she would do as she pleased.

"You are free to do as you like," Luke said, steeling himself against whatever angry words she might unleash on him—something he was also quite familiar with.

But Jane simply said, "Thank you," in a quiet voice and started across the lawn toward the house.

He had hoped they might have a discussion about their plan for the ball, how many dances they would dance together and whether they would dance with other people. He opened his mouth to call her back, but the thought of her anger stopped him.

Was he destined to compare every woman to Anne? Would he ever lose this dread of marrying someone who was angry and defiant and hated staying home?

He just had to get through the next few months, save Jane Gilchrist's reputation, and then he could figure out how to get past these bad memories and associations.

He hurried forward and caught up with Jane just before she opened the door to go back inside.

"Forgive me if I sounded like I was accusing you. What did the man look like? Do you remember?"

"Yes, he had dark hair with a bit of gray mixed in. He was rather thick in the chest, and he had a heavy brow. He looked to be around thirty-five or forty years old."

"That doesn't sound like any of our gardeners. I will go and speak with the groom and see if he saw the same man."

Jane nodded and went into the house without another word.

He sighed. Jane had been such a capable ally when they'd been kidnapped, attacking Lenoir and doing as well as any man would have done in the situation. He only wished they still had that same spirit of amiable cooperation between them.

He turned and stalked back toward the stable. It didn't matter. If he had to sacrifice Jane Gilchrist's amiability to do what was best for his son, and indeed, what was best for him, then so be it.

Chapter Fifteen

Jane went into the breakfast room, which was cool and dark in the early evening. No one was going to believe that she wanted to marry Luke if she didn't calm herself.

She closed her eyes and breathed in and out. Gradually her heart stopped racing and she was able to breathe normally again.

How will I get through this night without telling Luke Watley just what he can do with his pretend engagement?

When she was calm again, she was able to turn her attention to her skirt. Thankfully, she didn't see any mud on her hem, but her shoes were ruined. She went upstairs to change. In her room, she gazed at herself in the mirror. Truly, her hair was as well-looking as she'd ever seen it, her complexion was better than usual, and her dress was immaculate. If Luke Watley was not attracted to her tonight, then he never would be.

It was just as well. She'd feel vindicated that she hadn't run after the most sought-after man in England when she told everyone, in a few months, that she had called off their engagement. And even more when they saw that she was not sad or broken-hearted, but as happy and carefree as she had always been before she'd been unfortunate enough to be kidnapped with Luke Watley.

Back downstairs, Penelope motioned to her rather emphatically. "Guests are arriving," she said in a loud whisper as Jane hurried to stand beside Luke Watley as they greeted the first guests to their ball.

They had never made a formal announcement of their engagement, but greeting the guests together, side by side, was as good as a notice in the newspaper.

More than one mother and daughter bestowed snide looks at the pair of them, and several young ladies wore solemn and doleful expressions, their hopes of a match with young widower Luke Watley dashed.

Jane wanted to say, "He's all yours in a few months," but she refrained.

It was assumed that the first dance would be led by the host and his fiancée. Luke had not spoken to her about it, but when the guests had all arrived and the musicians were ready, Luke led her to the dance floor.

Her first glimpse of his expression as they faced each other, waiting for the music to start, told her that he was not enjoying himself. Then his eye met hers and he smiled, but the smile looked strained and insincere, and his gaze flitted around the room. Only when the music started did his gaze finally settle on her face.

"You look very lovely this evening," he said, but the usual warmth was absent from his tone.

"I thank you. And you look very handsome."

He raised his brows. She hoped he didn't think her compliment meant she cared for him. She was only making an observation and complimenting him as he had complimented her.

Jane had seen the guests watching them, even after the other couples joined the dance, so she did her best to keep a pleasant smile on her face. It was more difficult when Luke did not look especially pleasant.

She was glad when the dance was over and she could go to Penelope's side.

"Did we look like a happy engaged couple?" she whispered to Penelope.

"Do you want the truth?"

"Yes."

"Not very happy. But perhaps it's because I know you both so well."

"Lovely." Jane sighed and closed her eyes.

"Here comes Lady Ingraham," Penelope whispered, barely moving her lips.

"Jane." Sarah was smirking as she came toward her, holding her hands out to her.

"Sarah. I trust you are enjoying yourself." Jane's stomach sank. She'd nearly forgotten that Sarah would be one of the guests, as she and Lord Ingraham had a house in Hertfordshire.

"And I am most gratified to see you, Jane, and allow me to wish you every happiness in your upcoming marriage to Luke Watley, you sly thing."

Jane felt herself bristle at Sarah's "sly thing" remark. She didn't want to ask her what she meant, but she wouldn't be able to get past it if she didn't, so she said, "Must I be sly to land a husband?"

"You know what I meant. That ball two weeks ago, when you and I were standing above the fray, watching all the young women fawning over newly widowed Luke Watley. You and I remarked upon it, so above it all, and all the time . . . but perhaps I presume too much. Perhaps the two of you had no attachment at all at that time."

Jane was trapped. If she said there had been no attachment between her and Luke, she was admitting that they had become attached, in love, and engaged in less than two weeks' time—most likely while they were kidnapped. But if she said yes, they had indeed already formed an attachment before that night, then she would have to admit that she was rather sly in the fact that she had played along with Sarah as she made sport of the ladies' desperate attempts to get Luke's attention—when Jane had already arrested his attention for herself.

Why had she ever suggested this foolish charade?

"Either way, we are attached now," she said, smiling. And it wasn't untrue. They were attached by their agreement.

The next song started and Jane was surprised that Luke had not come to escort her to the dance floor. She glanced around and saw him speaking to a small group of men. By their expressions, they were discussing some political issue, such as the corn laws.

"I was hoping my brother Henry would be able to attend tonight, but his business in London must have prevented him." She was trying to distract herself as well as Sarah from the fact that her fiancé had not come to ask her to dance the second dance, as would have been customary.

"I heard about that terrible kidnapping. It is so very shocking. I suppose the kidnappers were hoping to get a ransom?"

"Yes. Fortunately, we escaped before they got what they wanted."

"It must have been harrowing. But having Luke Watley with you must have been a comfort." Her lip curled and one of her brows went up.

"Well, the fact that he had been knocked unconscious and was bleeding profusely rather precluded that comfort." Henry had told her she should take care not to reveal such details, especially to a gossip like Sarah, but she couldn't resist.

Sarah held a gloved hand up to her mouth, her eyes wide. "How shocking."

"But I know you would not wish to know about that. Truly, he was not seriously injured, in the end, and I was completely unhurt."

"That is a mercy," Sarah said, "but still, it is so very shocking. We are not safe on the streets of London anymore, it seems. But all turned out well for you." Again, she had that smirking smile on her face.

"Yes, indeed." Jane wondered how she might escape this conversation. "I believe I must check on the refreshments and make certain the servants do not need further instruction. Would you excuse me?"

"Of course. And let me—"

Jane hurried away before Sarah could finish her sentence, pretending not to know she was talking to her.

She must be getting accustomed to pretending. But that did not seem like a good thing.

It took only a few moments to make sure everything was proceeding smoothly with the refreshments and the food preparations. When she came back out to the ballroom, she noticed a group of three women staring at Luke a moment before they bent their heads and started whispering among themselves. No doubt they were wondering why he wasn't dancing with his fiancée.

Jane was wondering the same thing.

How could he humiliate her this way? It was the same as saying he cared nothing for her, that he would rather talk with the other men than dance with the woman he was supposed to be in love with. But then, so many marriages were made for reasons other than that the couple was in love. Was everyone assuming that Jane, after being so vocal about her opinions on marriage, that it should be for love and not a financial arrangement, had changed her mind and decided to marry to save her own reputation?

Jane felt her face heat.

If that was what everyone was thinking then she would call off the engagement here this very night. It wasn't real anyway, and she was already quite tired of it.

She went to look for Penelope before anyone should ask her a question, for she was at risk of snapping at anyone who spoke to her at this moment.

She finally spotted her approaching Luke. He stepped away from the small group of men and apparently had to bend down to hear her. Moments later, he straightened, looked around until he saw Jane, then strode toward her.

Jane could just imagine what Penelope had said to him. Something like, "Shouldn't you be dancing with your fiancé? Everyone is expecting it."

Penelope was so gentle and soft-spoken, everyone listened when she talked. But Jane was just the opposite. She could be quite loud and free with her opinions, and often she'd seen the taken-aback expression on people's faces when they thought she had shared her forward-thinking opinions too frankly.

Jane had accepted a long time ago that she wasn't the quiet, perfect image of a young lady that Society portrayed as the ideal, and she didn't want to be. Someone had to challenge the norms, did they not? There were too many women who were maltreated, hidden and downtrodden, with no good options for their future. It was a Christian's duty to defend the orphan and widow, but few people seemed to remember that.

Such strange thoughts to go through her head when Luke was coming toward her, his face serious and grim.

Before he could speak, she said, "You look as if you are on your way to your execution."

His face went slack, his mouth falling open slightly. "Forgive me." He leaned down and whispered, his breath tickling her ear, "Will you dance with me?"

When he lifted his head, he was smiling. But again, she hoped she was the only one who realized he was smiling with his lips but his heart was not in it.

They were able to join the dance that was just starting. Luke was an expert dancer and never seemed to miss a step. But she couldn't help remembering how he had gazed into her eyes at the last ball they'd attended, that fateful night. He'd made her feel as if he truly saw her, as if he was intrigued by her and was enjoying dancing with her.

At the moment he was looking into her eyes but she felt as if his thoughts were galloping here and there. He was dancing by rote, not with his senses. Why should that send a pain through her chest?

At the risk of looking like a fawning fool, Jane smiled brightly at Luke, glancing away, as if he'd said something that made her feel shy. When she looked back, he seemed to have taken the hint and his smile was bigger and less wooden.

When the dance was over, he walked her to where Penelope was sitting and asked, "Are you enjoying the ball?"

"As much as I can under the circumstances." She smiled as if she had said something witty.

"I am sorry I'm not very good at pretenses."

"It is not what I prefer either. But as long as we can get through the rest of the ball . . ." She stopped talking when she saw a mother and her daughter, who was in her second season, approach them.

"Allow me to wish you every happiness," the mother said, "as I hear you are engaged."

"Thank you very much," they both said.

"It is only a shame that you have no brothers for my daughter, Mr. Watley."

"Mamma!" Her daughter's face turned red.

"It is a shame indeed," Jane agreed, smiling, "as he would be quite handsome, judging from how handsome my Mr. Watley is." Jane laid a hand on Luke's arm, smiling as if she truly were in love.

"It is good to see a sensible match that is also a love match," the lady said, but Jane thought she noted a bit of artifice in her eyes, as if she were being insincere and doubting that they truly were in love.

They needed to be more convincing, but Jane felt a bit of panic fluttering inside her stomach. Did everyone know their engagement was not real? If so, Jane had to break it off. Was everyone laughing at her, seeing through their charade and clucking their tongues at Jane's hypocrisy?

"Shall we dance again?" Luke said, gazing down at her.

Jane nodded and turned to the mother and daughter. "Excuse us."

"Of course."

Jane let Luke lead her to the dance floor again. She

did her best to pretend joy and high spirits. She smiled and danced with a lively step, imagining what it would be like if she truly was in love and Luke was in love with her. As long as she believed it, on some level, she was able to keep smiling, to let her hand linger on Luke's hand or arm longer than necessary, and to throw flirty looks his way. She was flirting, truly flirting, something she rarely allowed herself to do, and never to this degree. And she found she rather liked it, as Luke became more attentive, more intense with his gazes, with every flirtatious smile and touch of her hand. How could she not enjoy it?

A feeling of guilt was also lurking, for it was wrong to lead a man to think she felt more for him than she did. But Luke had made her so angry, her guilt was short-lived.

Besides, she was doing what they had agreed to do, and he was so bad at pretending to be engaged that she had to play it up as best she could.

At least, that's what she was telling herself.

Chapter Sixteen

When the song ended, Jane took Luke's arm and said, "I think I will get some lemonade."

"I will get it for you," he said. "Wait here."

Penelope was speaking with an older gentleman and Jane was content to glance around at the crowd, wishing she had suggested to Luke that they dance the next dance together. Now that he was fetching her a cup of lemonade, she'd have to talk to him.

He brought her a cup, also carrying a cup for himself, and they stood side by side watching as the next dance began.

"You are a very good dancer," Jane said, carrying on with her plan as she smiled up at him, her lips touching the rim of her cup.

Luke's gaze was drawn to her mouth, and she saw his throat bob as he swallowed.

"You are a very capable dancer as well," he said.

Was he blushing?

"I thank you. Dancing is something I've always enjoyed. Do you enjoy it? Or is it only something you do because it's expected?"

"You always strike at the heart of things, don't you?" he said with a bit of a wry grin. "I mostly enjoy it, but I also do it because it's expected of a gentleman, as we are to assume that we are pleasing the lady by asking her to dance."

"Yes, that is what everyone assumes, and correctly, I daresay." Again, Jane made sure to smile and gaze at him with wide eyes. "And yes, I do like to strike at the heart of things without beating about the bush, hinting and vaguely implying things. Most conversations are dull beyond my patience and so I have to strike deep to get at anything worthwhile."

Luke was staring intently into her eyes now, leaning closer, as he said, "You are not like other women, Jane Gilchrist."

"I hope that is a compliment."

"It is, since most women—forgive me—are terribly uninteresting."

She laughed, a quick burst of mirth, and then her stomach flipped as she realized he was implying that she was terribly interesting.

"Well, I cannot prattle on and on about muslins and whether long sleeves are in fashion, even though I do work in a clothing shop. And if someone talks endlessly about the condition of the roads and how much it has rained this spring, my mind starts to wander and then I seem rude, which is not my intention."

"What do you like to talk of?"

"I suppose I like to talk of important things, such as how the last novel I read made me feel, especially if the other person has read the same novel, and I want to know how it made them feel. And about whether the Psalmist is being literal when he says, 'I will walk through the fire and not be burned,' and 'no weapon formed against me shall prosper.' Does that mean nothing bad will happen to me? For I know it cannot mean that."

Luke's blue eyes seemed to sparkle. "So those are the things that go through your head."

"Among other things, of course."

"What else do you like to talk about?"

"No, no. It is your turn to say what you like to talk about, Luke Watley," she said, addressing him by his first and last name as he had done to her moments before.

They were facing each other, standing quite close in a shadowy spot against the wall, which must have been why no one approached or interrupted them.

"I like to talk of . . . You will think it is all exceedingly dull."

"Nevertheless, you must tell me honestly, as I told you."

"Very well. I like to discuss political viewpoints, and I typically can see both sides of an argument. I discuss hunting, and farming tools and methods are interesting to me, as I like to help my tenants if I can. But I also like to discuss theology, what is meant by certain Bible passages, and the purpose of our lives while we are here."

He wasn't a feather-headed bumpkin who thought of nothing besides hunting and riding and gaming and where he might get his next drink of port. She supposed she'd always known that, but it was good to get confirmation.

It hardly mattered. But while she was pretending to be in love with him, it did matter, and it made it much easier to pretend.

The music was starting. She wondered if she should suggest that they dance again, since their conversation was making Jane's heart beat a little faster—

too fast for her own comfort. If she could feel so attracted to him such a short time after being angry with him, how was she to get through the next few months?

Luke had turned toward the dance floor, as if just noticing that a new dance was about to start, when a young gentleman approached. Luke introduced Jane to him and then they began to talk of when they might go on another hunt like the one where they shot fifteen pheasants between them.

Jane would not be dancing this one, as another gentleman approached and the three of them stood talking of some of the things Luke had said he enjoyed discussing—hunting, political viewpoints, and farming methods.

Penelope turned to Jane. "Everyone seems to be enjoying themselves. Are you?"

"I am." She smiled and took a sip of her lemonade. Everything was going as she'd hoped, even though Luke had not been very convincing in the beginning. They would need to dance a few more times, and look as if they were pleased to be in each other's company, to convince all the guests that they were in love.

Certainly, she shouldn't care so much. It was her reputation that was most important, if she ever wished to marry—and she did. But if she was honest, it was her pride that she was trying to protect by making everyone think she and Luke were in love. Otherwise people would laugh at her behind her back about all the times she'd said she would never marry unless it was for a deep and abiding love, and that she would never marry for money or social standing.

She watched as Luke drained his cup of lemonade and gave it to a passing servant while the men around him were obviously intent on their conversation, using their hands to punctuate their words. Luke was rather intent as well, until a middle-aged woman with rosy cheeks interrupted them. Jane heard her say, ". . . take your discussion away from the ballroom . . . dancing and merrymaking . . ."

"Don't go," Jane whispered under her breath, willing Luke to stay and play the loving fiancée, but he turned and led the gentlemen to a side where tables and card games were set up.

And he did not return.

Jane wanted to dance, but now she'd either have to pretend she didn't want to dance anymore, or find another partner, and the latter did not seem wise.

Jane would leave the ballroom before anyone else came to talk to her. If she disappeared at the same time as Luke, it wouldn't seem as if he had left her standing with the dancers while he went to talk politics with the other men. Most people would assume they were together.

She slipped from the room, and with each step she took toward the staircase, her anger grew. He'd left her standing there.

Why would his going into another room to talk with the men make her angry? She knew she was overreacting, but didn't he know that he was supposed to be dancing with her?

She was reminded of when she was a little girl. Her father had taken her with him to scout for pheasants. Jane was very young and had just learned to ride her own horse without help. They stopped their horses at a small stream where Jane was happily watching the tiny fishes just under the water.

"Wait here for me," her father said, taking out his

gun. "You can play in the stream while I go look for pheasants."

No doubt he hadn't wanted her to scare off the birds. She had played in the stream a long time, and when he didn't come back she rode home, getting lost once or twice but finally making it back.

When the groom came out and took her horse's reins, he gave her a surprised look, but Jane ran from the stable to the house and yelled to her mother, "Father is lost! He told me to wait at the stream but he didn't come back!"

Her mother and older brother ran out of the house, Jane just behind them, all the way to the stable. They told the grooms that Mr. Gilchrist was lost in the woods, and just as they were saddling horses to go look for him, her father came riding up toward the stable with a pair of pheasants tied to his saddle.

Her father suddenly saw Jane and his eyes widened, his brows shooting up. "Oh, Jane. Forgive me. I forgot all about you."

Mother looked horrified, her expression turning to anger.

Henry's mouth fell open, his eyes dolefully fastened on Father.

But the grooms were laughing. They laughed and laughed, ducking back into the stable to keep from being scolded, while Mother shook her finger at Father.

"She is just a little girl. She could have been hurt or lost! Or worse! How could you leave her alone and forget about her? I cannot believe it."

"You really came back all by yourself?" Henry said to Jane, patting her shoulder. "That's impressive for a little girl like you."

He was trying to tease her, to take her mind off the argument their parents were having, but Jane's heart was broken. Her father had forgotten about her. Did she not matter to him?

She'd tried to tell herself that their father might have taken Henry into the woods and forgotten about him, but she didn't believe it. Father would never have forgotten Henry. He had never, and he would never. But Jane was not as important in her father's eyes as his son was. She was just a girl so she didn't matter as much.

Father took Henry with him much more often than he took her. Father spoke to Henry more often than he did her. Father loved Henry more. She didn't know when she had come to that conclusion, she'd just always known it to be true.

And when he left her in the woods and forgot about her to go shoot pheasants, he had proven it not only to her but to her mother, Henry, and even the servants. How the grooms had laughed!

Her stomach sank at the humiliation of it. And it seemed as if Luke had just done the same thing in walking away with those men instead of staying in the ballroom and dancing with his fiancée. Again she felt the pain of people knowing she didn't matter to someone she loved.

Jane climbed the stairs slowly, her feet heavy. With all the noise of the ball below her, she felt alone, lonely, and unloved.

She was near the nursery and the door was slightly ajar. Jeffrey was crying, and she went to peek in on him.

Carefully, she approached the door. Sally was standing beside Jeffrey's bed and saying in a hushed voice, "No, you can't go downstairs, and your father can't come up here. He's very busy with the grown-up people. But I am here looking after you."

Jeffrey said in a whiny voice, "No. I want to go find Papa."

"You can't. It's nighttime and you're supposed to be abed, asleep."

Poor little lad. All the noise of the ball must have awakened him. Jane began to back away from the door, lest Jeffrey see her and start making even more of a fuss.

She took a step backward, then another, and bumped into something solid.

Spinning around, she found herself face to face with Luke.

Jane jumped in surprise. Thankfully, she stopped herself from screaming. Was she so afraid of him catching her looking in on his son? She raised her chin, wrapped her arms around herself, and looked him in the eye.

"Why were you sneaking up on me?" she whispered.

"I wasn't sneaking up on you," he whispered back. "I was coming to look in on Jeffrey."

At that moment, Sally shut the door. She didn't seem to see them standing a few feet away in the shadows of the hall.

"What were you doing lurking about outside his door?" he asked.

"Excuse me? Lurking about?" How dare he accuse her! "I was getting a bit of air and heard crying and— I don't have to explain myself to you." She turned and hurried away from him, back toward the stairs.

She was almost to the top step when she spun on her heel and said, "And if you don't wish to play this charade anymore, tell me now and we can inform our guests that we have no plans to marry."

He was still standing where she'd left him, staring back at her. She heard him let out an audible breath. "If you wish. It is your reputation that will suffer."

Her cheeks burned at his callous dismissal of her. He was making it clear that he didn't care at all.

Jane hurried down the stairs, unable to make a civil reply. Indeed, she wasn't sure what to say. And telling their guests that they were no longer engaged—or that they never were—felt too humiliating.

Someone else was on the stairs below her, moving fast. Had they heard what she'd said about their charade? About informing their guests that they had no plans to marry?

As she reached the bottom, a woman moved toward the light of the ballroom. It was Sarah.

Jane's heart sank to her toes. What should she do now? Sarah would surely tell everyone what she'd heard, and in a few minutes half the room would know that they were not actually engaged.

Perhaps Sarah hadn't heard—Jane had been whispering. But her sinking feeling, and the way Sarah had hurried down the stairs, told Jane that she had.

She should probably go back up the stairs and tell Luke, discuss with him what they should do. But the very thought of speaking to him made her blood boil. She wished she never had to speak to him again.

Back in the ballroom, she went to stand beside Penelope, who turned to her and asked, "What is the matter?"

"Nothing is the matter. I want to dance."

A young man was looking at her from across the room. She'd been introduced to him when they were welcoming their guests, but Jane couldn't remember his name.

Jane smiled at him, giving him what she hoped was a long and inviting look, then turned her gaze aside. A moment later, she saw from the corner of her eye that he was coming toward her.

"Miss Gilchrist. Would you do me the honor of dancing with me?"

"Of course." She laid her hand on his arm and walked with him to the dance floor, spying Luke just entering the room. He stopped. One glance told her he was watching her and her dance partner.

Jane smiled at her partner as brightly as she could. He turned a shade of red and smiled back.

She danced and flirted with the young man—she wished she could remember his name—and did her best to forget that she was supposed to be engaged to a man who made her so angry that for a minute she literally saw everything through a film of red.

When the dance ended, she glanced around the room but didn't see Luke. But it was just as well. What she did see was Sarah whispering with two other ladies. They were so intent on what Sarah was saying that they did not notice Jane looking at them.

She went on smiling and soon another young man asked her to dance. She ended up dancing several more dances, smiling and determined to enjoy herself.

Luke suddenly appeared when the ball was nearly over. "May I have the last dance?" he asked.

"Yes, of course," she said. She did her best to make conversation with Penelope while she waited for the last dance to start. What would Luke say? Would he be angry with her for dancing and flirting with every unmarried man in the room? He shouldn't, since he didn't care about her. Would he tell her he wished to inform everyone they were not engaged?

Her heart beat fast, practically jumping into her throat.

"My dear, when the ball is over, please talk to me and tell me what's wrong," Penelope said.

"Very well." Jane could never deny Penelope anything she asked for, as she never asked for too much and was so generous herself. Besides, she knew Penelope genuinely cared about her.

Before the last dance Luke came and claimed her. As they started toward the dance floor, she tried to read his expression. Was he angry? Embarrassed by her behavior? Did all of her flirting remind him of his first wife?

Needles pricked her skin as the blood drained from her face. How similar her behavior must seem to Anne's.

How he must despise her. And how glad he must be that they were not actually engaged to be married.

As they danced, not speaking, part of her wanted to apologize to him. But then she remembered how cold he had been when he'd accused her of *lurking* outside Jeffrey's room and when he'd told her it would be her reputation that would suffer.

Her cheeks heated. She was glad she had danced with the other gentlemen. Luke obviously didn't care about her, didn't want her, didn't care to dance with her. He probably only asked to dance with her now to show that it wasn't his fault if people thought they weren't in love. He could blame it all on her if people discovered the truth.

Chapter Seventeen

Jane was dancing with Luke, but she wished she was back in London adding and subtracting numbers and filing away the shop's receipts. Numbers didn't upset her. They never confused her or made her question herself or her motives. They were what they were and they didn't change.

In her office, in her own little chair, all was predictable and safe.

But it wasn't like her to want predictability and safety, not all the time. She wanted to gallop across the countryside, visit the ocean and its crashing waves, see things she hadn't seen before. She wanted . . . something she couldn't have—the love of a good man.

Luke was staring down at her as if he wanted to say something. "There is some gossip," he said, or at least, that's what she thought he said. His voice was so low it was barely audible.

"Gossip?"

"About us. There is talk that we are not, in fact, engaged at all."

"Who is saying that?"

"My friend told me he overheard some ladies speaking of it."

"I think Lady Ingraham heard what I said to you in the hall outside the nursery." She wanted to say she was sorry, that she had been foolish to say what she did, especially where someone might hear. But her pride held her back.

She was about to ask him what he thought they should do, but the music ended and so did the dance.

The servants were already moving to place tables and chairs on the dance floor and all around the ballroom. In very little time, the room would be turned into a large dining hall and filled with conversation instead of dance music.

Before Jane could try to talk to Luke, an older gentleman came to talk to him, and Jane went to find Penelope.

The rest of the evening, Luke was surrounded by guests, and he often looked deep in conversation. Jane stayed near Penelope, trying to look as if she was enjoying herself, talking with the people sitting around her.

The woman who had been sitting next to Jane vacated her seat and Lydia Newman, a long-time acquaintance of Jane's, took her place.

"So, Jane, tell me the truth. Are you and Luke Watley actually engaged to be married? For there is a rumor that you are only pretending."

"Aren't you the brave one, Lydia." Jane stared her in the eyes.

"It is only a rumor, probably invented by someone who is jealous of you landing the gentleman we were all madly in love with a fortnight ago. But is it true?"

"People will believe what they want to believe, no matter what I say. So I will not tell you. Let each person make up his own mind."

Lydia leaned toward her. "Will you not tell me the truth?"

"I will not. Believe what you wish." Jane smiled.

Lydia shook her head. Then she whispered, "I am hoping you're not engaged, because I want to marry him."

Jane just smiled. "He is handsome, isn't he?"

They both turned to look at Luke, who was sitting at a table several feet away. He noticed them looking at him and stopped in the middle of what he was saying to stare back at them, his mouth hanging slightly open.

"Yes, he is," Lydia said, then sighed. "If you don't want him, I do."

They both laughed, even as a pain stabbed Jane's middle. Luke didn't want her, and she wasn't even sure if she wanted him. The only reason she was continuing with the charade was because he was risking his reputation as well.

Lydia left, no doubt to go back to the other ladies and report what Jane had said. The woman across the table remarked to her about how good Dunsmere House's cooks were and complimented the food, and soon Jane was talking with the others around her as they spoke of the lovely grounds, the beauty of the house, and the varied society in Hertfordshire.

"One could not do better than Luke Watley," the older woman said. "And he is quite handsome. I hear his son looks exactly like he did when he was a child."

The woman was being very kind, as some had speculated on the doubt of Luke being Jeffrey's father, since it was known that Anne had not been faithful. But the truth was, Jeffrey did look very much like Luke, with the same color eyes and even the same facial structure. He was a handsome little boy.

"They do look very much alike." Jane smiled. *Even if Luke doesn't wish me to spend time with Jeffrey.* She mustn't let bitterness take root, but she couldn't help feeling defensive.

Overall, Jane was enjoying herself, even knowing that everyone was gossiping and speculating about her engagement to Luke. If she was honest with herself, she liked pretending that he was her fiancé and that they were engaged to be married. No doubt, she'd have to deal with the consequences of those feelings later, but for now, she was Luke Watley's fiancée.

~ ~ ~

Luke caught Jane and Lydia Newman staring, obviously talking about him. He told himself he didn't care, but he did wonder what they were saying as they were smiling and looking sneaky. But he knew Jane hated him now, after he had told her, although not in so many words, to stay away from Jeffrey.

He hated fighting with her, as it always reminded him of his relationship with Anne. And when she'd gone and started dancing with every man at the ball, he'd felt an actual stab in his heart, remembering how Anne had lashed out at him by showing interest in other men, acting as if she wasn't even married.

And then, of course, there was the affair with Lenoir, as well as rumored affairs with one or two others.

He could never marry Jane. That was clear enough. But he was also seeing how much he might overreact in certain situations if he did marry again. If his new wife innocently danced with another man, which was certainly not uncommon, Luke would probably want to accuse his wife of contemplating being unfaithful. Such a thing would be an overreaction and not conducive to a healthy relationship.

Or if his new wife argued with him, he'd feel convinced that she was like Anne, contentious and impossible to get along with, when in fact arguing was inevitable for two people in a close relationship. And he did wish for a close relationship with his wife, something he'd longed for but had not attained with Anne, who was constantly pushing him away.

He knew of some traumatic events from her childhood, but she had become angry if he tried to talk to her about them, accusing him of all manner of things, when he just wanted to know her better, to know how she felt and thought. But those were obviously things she did not want.

Sometimes Luke was convinced that Jane could be that woman he'd always longed for, an intelligent partner who would share her thoughts and feelings with him, and to whom he could share his thoughts and feelings—his life. But he had a terrible suspicion that he had been pushing her away just as Anne had done to him.

Lydia Newman went to sit behind him at her own table, and even though his friend Tom Kennemer was talking to him, he heard Lydia say, "I asked Jane if she and Mr. Watley were really engaged, and she just smiled and said, 'He is handsome, isn't he?' What do you make of that?"

He didn't hear her companion's reply as he mulled over Jane's answer. She hadn't lied about their engagement, and she hadn't revealed the truth either. But it was ridiculous how much his insides warmed at Jane saying that he was handsome. His neck heated.

She was playing her part in this charade, nothing more. She disliked him, he was sure of it, and he couldn't blame her. So why did he even care if she thought he was handsome?

He didn't care. He wouldn't care. He couldn't.

He and his guests ate and drank until the early morning hours. Finally, some of them began to depart for home, so Luke positioned himself near the front door to bid them farewell.

He'd been there for several minutes but Jane had not joined him. Was she too angry with him to stand close to him and pretend they were in love?

"Thank you for coming," Luke said as he shook Mr. Simpson's hand. "I'm glad you enjoyed the evening," he replied to the man's compliments.

"You be good to that pretty fiancée of yours," old Mr. Simpson said, winking. "She looks spirited, and she's from a good family—neighbors of mine. Known them my whole life. You could not do better than Jane Gilchrist." He shook his finger at Luke's nose.

"Yes, sir. I know, sir." Luke smiled, but his contradictory thoughts made his stomach feel sick.

Suddenly, he heard a yell from the stairs above them.

His blood went cold in his veins. Instantly there came a piercing scream. It sounded like Sally, coming from Jeffrey's nursery.

Blood surging through his limbs, Luke turned and bolted toward the stairs.

~ ~ ~

Jane wasn't sure she was equal to the task of bidding farewell to their guests, not after the last tiff with Luke. She already regretted what she'd said—except when she wished she'd said even more. Her emotions swung one way one moment and the opposite way the next.

As the guests began to leave, she quietly slipped away and started up the stairs, which were empty, as the servants were still busy downstairs and the guests were making their way to the front door.

The stairs were dimly lit and Jane was breathing deeply, enjoying a bit of solitude after so many conversations with so many people. Suddenly she heard a hoarse whisper above her.

Glancing up, she saw a man hurrying along the landing toward the nursery, while a second man entered her bedroom.

Jane ran up the last few stairs, yelling at the man as he reached the nursery door. "What are you doing there?"

The man glared at her, then opened the door.

Jane lunged at him. Inside the nursery, Sally screamed. Jeffrey started crying.

Jane caught hold of the man's collar and yanked, which jerked his head back. He made a gagging sound and clutched at his collar. He quickly pivoted and broke her grip with a sweep of his arm.

With his meaty hand, he grabbed her by the throat, cutting off her air with a bruising hold on her neck.

Jane was dimly aware of feet pounding up the steps behind her. She wanted to shout but it was impossible, with no breath able to pass through her throat. Black spots were already entering her vision, and her face and limbs were tingling and going numb.

But just as the blackness was closing in, he loosened his grip enough that she was able to breathe again. Somehow she was able to keep her feet under her as the man let go and turned her around, now wrapping his arm around her neck.

Chapter Eighteen

"Unhand her!" Luke's heart pounded at seeing the large and menacing man holding Jane by the throat. He ran toward them.

The man spun Jane around and wrapped his arm around her neck, so that she was facing Luke.

"Stop or I'll break her neck!" he said.

Luke froze, as did the handful of other gentlemen just behind him.

"Let her go and leave." Luke clenched his jaw, his gaze moving back and forth between Jane's face and her captor's.

"So if I let her go, I can leave?" The man's tone matched his sneer.

Luke was trying to decide what to do to keep both Jane and Jeffrey safe. If the fiend let Jane go, no doubt he would go into the nursery and use Jeffrey to get away. He had to act wisely. After all, this man would not hesitate to murder Jane and even Jeffrey if it served his purposes.

Suddenly, Jane shifted her body to one side and used her fist to punch the man in the groin. He grunted and loosened his hold around her neck, enabling her to spin around and use her knee to really hurt him.

The man let go of her as he hunched over, making

gasping noises.

Jane stepped away as Luke rushed forward and knocked the man to the floor on his face. The other men surrounded him as a middle-aged gentleman sat on his back, another gentleman pinning his hands behind him.

A footman arrived at the top of the stairs. "Fetch some rope," Luke said. He almost sent another servant to fetch the constable. But perhaps he could get more information without the constable or Justice of the Peace.

The other gentlemen and one footman were searching the intruder's pockets and person for weapons, which produced two knives in quick succession. They seemed to have matters under control.

Jane was standing against the wall, hugging herself and staring at the man who had just attacked her. Luke leaned toward her, his eyes roving over her face and resting on her neck, where purple bruises were already appearing.

"Are you all right? I'm so sorry."

His chest clenched painfully. How could he have let this happen? Once again, Jane had come in harm's way because of him.

~ ~ ~

In all the excitement and her fear that the man would escape into the nursery and harm Jeffrey, Jane was just now becoming aware of the pain in her throat. She could still feel where the man's fingers had gouged into her flesh.

"I am well," Jane rasped, wincing at how painful it was to speak. She kept swallowing, but that didn't help.

"What can I do?" Luke looked up. "Mrs. Gilchrist." He motioned Penelope over to them.

"Oh, my dear," Penelope said. "They told me what

happened. Let me take care of you."

"Wait." Jane grabbed Luke's arm. "Another man. He went in my room."

Luke said, "Stay here."

He stepped away, motioned to the two footmen and a groom who were coming up the stairs with the rope, and leaned in to speak to the men in a low voice. One of them took the rope to the men who were holding Jane's assailant, while Luke and the other two went toward Jane's room.

Penelope was saying, "Darling, are you all right? What a horrible fright. How badly are you hurt?"

"Just my throat." She strained to see what Luke and the servants would find in her room and started walking that way.

"Luke said to stay here." Penelope laid a gentle hand on Jane's arm.

Jane wanted to say, "Don't worry," but her throat hurt so much and her voice sounded so hoarse that she only nodded at Penelope and motioned to her in a way she hoped would reassure her as she moved slowly toward her bedroom door.

The men had gone inside. All was quiet as Jane moved closer to peer into her open door.

The curtain at the window was fluttering from a slight breeze, so the window must be open. She could see shadowy figures moving around.

Finally Luke came out and said, "He must have gone, probably out the window." He took her gently by the arm. "I will send for the apothecary."

"Thank you."

"Truly, you sound very bad." Luke frowned.

"I'll go for the apothecary," a young man said, one

of the ones Jane had danced with when she was angry with Luke.

Luke said nothing for a moment, then, "Tell him Miss Gilchrist has a sore throat but that it's from an injury to the front of her neck. Her voice is hoarse and she is in pain."

The young man nodded and bolted away.

Luke was still staring down at her as everyone else seemed to be rushing to and fro or scolding the man they were tying up. His hand was warm and gentle on her upper arm, a familiarity that he would not be allowed if he were not her supposed fiancé.

"I know you to be very brave," Luke said quietly so no one else could hear, "but even you must feel a bit shaken. What happened?" His voice was low and gruff as he brought his face even with hers.

Her heart skittered and skipped at his concern. No one seemed to notice them standing alone outside her room, having a private conversation. Even Penelope seemed to have wandered away.

"You shouldn't talk," he said. "I don't want you to hurt your throat by talking. But you were trying to prevent that man from going into the nursery, weren't you?"

She nodded.

"Jane." He said her name on a burst of air, a cross between a whisper and a groan. "You saved my son." His voice sounded as if he were holding back tears. But men didn't cry, did they? But then she remembered what Henry had said about Luke after his wife was killed, about how he had never seen a man more affected.

The poor man. He had been through more than his share of troubles. Thanks be to God, she had been there to stop his son from being kidnapped.

He put a hand up to his mouth and closed his eyes for a moment, but it was too dark in the hallway for her to see his expression clearly. Then she heard him take a deep breath and let it out slowly.

"Thank you, Jane. Thank you for saving Jeffrey."

Jane said haltingly, "I would do . . . anything . . . for him."

He leaned even closer, as if to block other people's view, and took her hand in his. He lifted it to his lips and kissed it.

Jane's stomach fluttered like the window curtain. She imagined him kissing her lips instead of her hand.

"I will check on you later, but I must go now."

Jane nodded.

"Will you stay in your sister-in-law's room tonight?"

Jane nodded again. Truthfully, she wasn't very eager to sleep in the room where one of those evil men had been only minutes before.

Luke looked as if he might say something else, but then he turned and strode away, asking a few men to go with him to search the grounds around the house. Then he was hurrying down the stairs, the others trailing behind him.

~ ~ ~

Dawn was breaking when the young man came back with the apothecary's remedy for Jane's sore throat. Luke thanked him and sent the overly helpful young man home, a bit of an urge to box his ears alerting Luke to his own jealousy as he remembered him dancing with Jane.

Luke wanted to take the bottle of medicine to Jane himself, but he didn't wish to wake her or Penelope or

Lilith, who slept in the room with her.

He was standing outside the room with the bottle in his hand when the door to Jane's room, which was next door, opened and Jane emerged.

She jumped, obviously startled to see him standing in the hall.

"Forgive me," he said. "I didn't mean to frighten you. I have the apothecary's remedy for your throat."

"Just fetching . . . something." She wadded up a flimsy piece of cloth, no doubt her nightgown, hiding it as best she could.

Suddenly, he wished he could see her in that flimsy nightgown. But that was unchivalrous. What was wrong with him? Obviously it had been too long since . . . But he shouldn't let his mind go there.

He held the bottle out to her. "One small draft every two hours. It should soothe your throat until it can heal."

Jane nodded. She reached out to take the bottle and their fingers touched. She did not snatch her hand away, but let her fingers linger on his. Or perhaps he was imagining that she did that. Perhaps he was the one who was reluctant to let the bottle go and break the connection.

But it didn't matter. They weren't actually engaged —he had to keep reminding himself.

"Did you find anything?" Jane rasped, her voice still quite hoarse.

"No. The man must have gotten away. We found evidence of a couple of horses that had been tethered in a stand of trees near the house. That must be how the man's cohort made his escape."

She was staring at his face. The only light was the pale edge of dawn, what little was able to make its way into the dark hall, and in it her face had an ethereal glow. Her brows were delicate arches, and her lips . . . he could easily imagine kissing them.

"And the other?" She was speaking of the man who had harmed her, but by her expression and the tone of her voice, she was thinking of something else entirely. And she was staring at his mouth.

"My grooms are holding him in the basement, and I've stationed one of Henry's guards outside the nursery door and the other on the grounds outside."

He was barely aware of the words he was saying as he gazed down at her. What excuse could he give for putting his arms around her and holding her?

"Are you cold?" he asked.

"Cold?" She was still staring at his lips. "No."

Was she getting closer? Standing on her tiptoes?

His heart was thumping hard. But under no circumstances would he ever kiss Jane Gilchrist. She was flighty, given to emotional outbursts, independent, didn't care what Society thought of her, and . . . she was the bravest, loveliest creature in the whole of England.

He leaned down. He would not kiss her. He was no selfish cad, kissing young ladies who didn't wish to be kissed. But if she kissed him . . .

"What happens now?" she said softly, her eyelids hanging low over her lovely eyes.

"I—" He had to stop and swallow the lump in his throat. "I think it best if we all go back to London. We obviously aren't as safe here as I'd hoped, and . . ." He lost his train of thought for a moment, trying to look away from her lips, every curve of her face melting his insides. "And Henry and I can try to figure out what it is these men are after."

"Oh. Good idea."

He could see her lovely throat move ever so slightly as she swallowed.

"I should go." She glanced over her shoulder, toward Penelope's room.

"Yes, I don't want you to get cold, and you will want to take your medicine. Forgive me for keeping you standing in the hall."

"I don't mind." She stepped toward him, slipped her arms around him, and laid her cheek against his chest.

His breath caught in his throat. He wrapped his arms around her.

This was something new and different. Anne never did anything so vulnerable, so . . . human. And it took his breath away to have the brave, independent, and beautiful Jane Gilchrist embrace him as if she was seeking his comfort.

"My brave girl," he whispered. The feel of her in his arms, her cheek pressed against him, made him wonder if he was dreaming. He wasn't sure if she could even hear him, but he said, "I will not let anyone harm you. I will keep you safe."

She didn't move for several more moments, then she raised her head, her eyes glistening.

Her gaze locked with his as if she were trying to read his thoughts, to feel what he was feeling. She put her hand on his shoulder, leaned forward, and their lips met in a gentle kiss.

Luke's heart beat double-time and he intensified the kiss, reveling not only in her willingness, but also in her obvious inexperience. As he kissed her slowly and deliberately, he gave her the freedom to pull away. And yet she continued to kiss him, holding onto him, intense emotion in the way she kissed him back.

He could feel his ardor rising, his emotions swirling. But then she leaned away, breaking the kiss. He felt the loss of her warmth as a shudder passed over his shoulders. But he told himself it was a good thing they stopped when they did.

Her eyes were big and luminous as she stared up at him. She backed away from him—one step, two, then three.

His arms ached to pull her back in, but he forced them down by his sides.

Did she regret their kiss? The grimace on her face, as if she was about to apologize, made his chest feel hollow.

Jane pressed the wadded-up nightgown and bottle to her chest as she continued to back away from him. "Good night," she said, and turned and went into her sister-in-law's room.

Luke closed his eyes and rubbed a hand over his face. Had he behaved badly, kissing an innocent young lady? He should have pushed her away, avoided her kiss, as he surely could have. But if he was honest with himself, he'd wanted to do more than just kiss her.

Jane Gilchrist had kissed him.

A new feeling of joy crowded out any regret. *Jane* kissed *him*. She'd come willingly into his arms, laid her head against him, and then kissed him.

He couldn't remember the last time he'd felt so hopeful.

Footsteps sounded on the stairs behind him. That would be one of his men coming to report to him.

He couldn't stand there reveling in Jane's kiss. The man who might have harmed his son—and did harm Jane

—was two floors below him, the only link and possibility of finding out what Lenoir was after.

Luke pushed all thoughts of Jane and the kiss from his mind. He'd worry about the consequences of it later. Now that he had made Dunsmere House as secure as possible, he needed to find out whatever he could, and by whatever means necessary, from their prisoner.

~ ~ ~

Jane lay wide awake remembering over and over the encounter with Luke, while Penelope and Lilith slept soundly nearby.

The events of the evening had played out as if Jane was watching it happen to someone else—actors on stage, a play she was watching. While she was being attacked, she'd hardly even felt much fear, her thoughts focused on how to escape. Afterward, she was vigilant, watching to make sure the man who had attacked her was securely captured and the other intruder she had seen was long gone.

Penelope had gotten Lilith back to sleep, then they talked a bit about what happened. When Jane saw Penelope stifle a yawn, she'd left the room to get her nightgown.

Luke startled her when she came out of her room, and she'd suddenly felt all the fright sweep over her that she'd avoided until that moment. Seeing him looking so tall and strong and protective, making sure she had the apothecary's medicine for her throat, she'd felt an overwhelming urge to go to him and embrace him as her fiancé. She wanted to stop feeling the evil man's hands on her throat and instead feel Luke's arms around her, comforting her, holding her until the tremble inside her subsided.

Perhaps it had been unwise, but she did just that. And it felt as heavenly as she'd imagined. But why had she kissed him? Her cheeks were still warm as she wondered what he must think of her.

When she'd returned to Penelope's room with the bottle of medicine and her nightgown, Penelope was sound asleep, and Jane was not about to wake her up, even though she wanted to tell her what had happened and try to make sense of it.

As Jane lay in bed, unable to sleep, she tried to remember what she'd been thinking just before she kissed Luke, when she had looked up at him. He'd had such a vulnerable look on his face, and she imagined kissing him. And then she did.

It probably wasn't as simple as that. But she'd never been one to ruminate overmuch on regrets.

She also couldn't honestly say she regretted kissing him.

But how would she feel when she saw him again in the harsh light of day, after all the things they'd said to each other and the way she'd danced with all the other men at the ball?

And then she had deliberately pressed her lips to his. Had her brazen behavior reminded him of Anne?

That was the last thing Jane wanted but now, with a horrible sinking feeling in the pit of her stomach, she was sure her behavior had done just that.

No respectable lady would ever kiss a gentleman on the lips that she wasn't even engaged to. Even Jane had never thought she would do such a thing, though she was rather independent and unconcerned with following rules just for the sake of rule-following. But she was scandalized at her own behavior.

She forced out a breath. It wasn't as if she had broken a direct commandment. She had only kissed a man. And he hadn't seemed to mind.

The memory of how Luke had instantly responded to her kiss made her wonder if he'd already been thinking of kissing her. As the kiss turned her stomach inside out, the thought that passed through her mind was, *He certainly seems to know what he's doing.*

The same fluttery feeling returned as she relived the kiss. She was surprised to find herself smiling at the memory, even as her face heated.

Suddenly Jane didn't want to talk it over with Penelope. She wanted to keep the memory fresh and safe from the scrutiny of anyone else. That way, even when she and Luke revealed that they were not engaged, she'd always be able to hold the memory of their kiss close to her heart, like a secret wish.

Chapter Nineteen

Luke stood before the man who had so brutally bruised Jane's neck with his rough hands and glared at him, his arms crossed. Two of his grooms stood by, looking as if they would be glad to punch him into unconsciousness.

"What is your name?" Luke asked.

The man only sneered, contempt emanating from his expression.

"Shall I loosen his tongue?" Matthews asked. The groom slammed his clenched fist into his own palm.

Luke didn't say anything, keeping his eyes on the ruffian to gauge his reaction. Finally, the man gave a half frown and said between clenched teeth, "They call me Stokes."

"Is that your name?"

"Aye." He grinned, making Luke doubt his veracity.

"So, Stokes, why did you come into my home?"

"I was to take your son back to Lenoir. I do as Lenoir says, as he pays me well." He ran his tongue over his front teeth, one of which was brown with decay and appeared cracked.

"What does Lenoir want with my son?"

"To hold him until he gets what he wants from

you."

"What is it Lenoir wants from me?"

"You would like to know that, would ye not?" Stokes laughed, an ugly chuckle.

"Is there something my wife took from him, something he's looking for?"

"What she took from him?" He laughed again, this time louder and longer.

Luke nodded at Matthews and the groom smacked Stokes in the back of the head.

"You would strike a man with his hands tied? That's not very gentlemanlike." Stokes grinned.

"You deserve far worse." Luke made sure to look as unconcerned for the man's welfare as possible. "I will give you another chance. What were Lenoir's men searching for in my home in London?"

Stokes said nothing.

Luke gave Matthews another nod and he smacked the back of the man's head again, just as Luke had instructed Matthews to do beforehand.

"I can do this all day," Stokes said with an arrogant look.

"But the next blows will be worse. Are you sure your loyalty to Lenoir is worth it? It is only a matter of time before we capture him. There are many men searching in London and elsewhere. We will find him, and then he will be executed for the murder of my wife." Luke forced himself to show no emotion, to feel nothing.

"What is that to me? Let them find him. Let them execute him."

"If you help us, then you might not be executed along with him."

Luke imagined he could see the man's thoughts

churning as his expression went blank.

"You will not get away, and there will be no exchanges of kidnapped persons for you."

"I'll take my chances."

"Tell me what Lenoir was looking for. He told me there was a list. A list of what?"

The man's contemptuous grin returned while his lips remained clamped shut.

Luke nodded at Matthews. He moved in front of Stokes and slammed his fist into his face.

Luke's mind kept going to thoughts of Anne being trampled and run over, then to how this man had hurt Jane, just as he'd wanted to take Jeffrey from his bed to terrify Luke's innocent child. And he did not feel sorry for letting Matthews punch the man.

Matthews shook his hand.

"Is that the best you can do?" Stokes said, his voice an angry growl as blood appeared on his lip.

"I'm just getting started," Matthews said.

"These two men don't like that you came into Dunsmere House and harmed an innocent lady," Luke said calmly. "They will be glad to cut off your fingers and toes one by one until you bleed out."

That was certainly not something they had even spoken about, but the two grooms kept up Luke's bluff by grinning, as if in anticipation.

"Now, since we can do this all day, or you can give us the information we want, tell us what you and Lenoir's other men were looking for in my home."

Stokes said nothing, but the arrogant expression was gone. After several moments Luke nodded again at Matthews.

As Matthews came around in front of Stokes, the

groom casually pulled a knife out of his pocket.

Luke would have to stop him before he actually cut the man's finger off, but he planned to wait until the last possible moment.

"Wait, wait. I'll tell you," Stokes said.

Matthews gave a sly half grin as he looked back at Luke.

Good job, Matthews.

Luke held up a hand. "Very well. Tell me."

"Your wife told Lenoir she had a list of names of all the people who were in Lenoir's pocket, including a couple of Members of Parliament, constables, JPs, and the like."

"Why did she make this list?" Luke tamped down the emotion rising from his gut. He had to steel himself.

"She was blackmailing Lenoir with it. She must of wanted out, but she never should'a' told Lenoir about that list."

"The people were in Lenoir's pocket, you say. Does that mean they wanted to overthrow the government?"

"I don't know nothing else. I told you what you wanted to know, now let me go."

"Gag him," Luke said, nodding at the other groom.

Stokes began to curse and struggle with his bonds, but since he was tied hand and foot, he could barely move, and his curses were soon muffled by the piece of cloth in his mouth that was being tied behind his head.

Luke walked out of the room, leaving the two grooms to guard the man who had squealed like a pig when he was threatened with having all his toes and fingers cut off.

Later Luke might deal with some guilt when he thought about what he'd done, and what he'd asked

Matthews to do—although Matthews had seemed quite eager to comply and probably enjoyed hitting a man who had assaulted a lady. But for now he couldn't feel any remorse. Instead, his mind was filled with the new thought that Anne had tried to get away from Lenoir. Had she realized she loved Luke and Jeffrey and wanted to be faithful to them? Or had she simply grown sick of Lenoir and his evil intentions?

He might never know, but somehow this new knowledge made everything seem better—and worse, since he realized that he would probably never know the full truth about his wife's motives and actions.

But as he headed up the stairs and instructed a servant to send for the constable, he knew he had to find that list before Lenoir and his men could get their hands on it.

He went straight to Anne's room and tore through all her drawers, all the nooks and crannies of her bedroom and adjoining dressing room, every piece of furniture. He even pulled her mattress off her bed, but he found nothing. But even as he searched, he knew she'd most likely have made the list, and hidden it, while she was in London, as she'd been there the last three or four months before her death.

He'd already decided that they all needed to return to London, since they obviously weren't safe from Lenoir here at his country estate. He hated to wake Jane or Penelope, considering they'd had, at most, two or three hours of sleep, but he felt responsible for them all—and for Jeffrey, who almost certainly would have been kidnapped if not for Jane's intervention.

He went and found the housekeeper.

"Tell Mrs. Gilchrist's and Miss Gilchrist's servants

that we must all be packed and ready to depart for London as soon as possible. I won't leave anyone behind, as I cannot ensure their safety if they stay here. Jeffrey and Sally must also come with me. I shall leave the grooms and footmen in charge of the household's safety and have them guard the perimeter of the house."

"Yes, sir." The housekeeper looked quite tired, and inwardly he vowed to give all the servants a bonus in their wages.

He hurried up the stairs to get his valet started packing their things and to search his own room, and elsewhere in the house, for the list.

~ ~ ~

The next morning Jane's throat and voice were a bit better. However, her eyes burned from getting only about an hour of sleep. But she wouldn't complain, as they were all sacrificing sleep to travel back to London. She knew Luke must have a good reason, but the only explanation she'd heard was that it wasn't safe for them any longer to stay in Hertfordshire, and that the master wished his guests to return to London.

As Jane, Penelope, the two young children, and their nurses all crowded into one carriage, Luke and the two guards rode alongside them on horseback.

Luke was giving last-minute instructions to the servants and guards, so Jane still had not spoken to him since their kiss. She'd wondered how awkward it would be, riding together in the carriage all the way to London, but their meeting was postponed now that he was riding on horseback.

Everyone's eyes were either bloodshot or puffy from lack of sleep, but blessedly, the children cried very little and slept most of the way. Even Jane, who rarely did so, dozed off for perhaps half an hour with her head on her folded-up cloak, leaning against the side of the carriage. Penelope also slept a bit while the two nurses occupied the children with toys and games, when they weren't sleeping.

When they finally reached London, it was growing dark and a light, cold rain was falling.

Luke was waiting to hand them out of the carriage. He gazed into Jane's eyes and said, "I'll make sure all is well and the guards are on duty, and then I'll pay a visit to Henry."

Jane and Penelope nodded. "Please be careful," Jane said.

His expression softened. "I shall." Then he mounted his horse and was gone.

~ ~ ~

Jane did not get as much work done the next day after walking to the shop with one of the guards. She found herself staring at the wall, her mind wandering. And when there was a lull in customers, Jane ended up telling Catherine about her adventures in Hertfordshire.

"That sounds terrifying! But you haven't told me anything about your . . ." Catherine glanced over her shoulder, then whispered, "your pretend engagement with Luke Watley."

Jane sighed. How much should she tell? Her mind immediately went to their kiss. She definitely shouldn't tell Catherine about that. Jane still didn't quite understand why she had done it, and sweet, proper Catherine would be shocked.

"Something happened!" Catherine said in a loud whisper. "What? What happened?"

"We quarreled a bit." Jane chewed on her lip. "I

danced with nearly every unmarried gentleman at the ball, mostly because I was angry with him."

"Oh, Jane, you didn't!"

"But then . . . I suppose I regretted doing that, just a bit."

"Did you speak to him about it? Did you say you were sorry?" Catherine asked.

"No. But I think he . . . perhaps . . . forgives me."

"Why? Because you saved his son from being kidnapped? I should think he was extremely grateful for that. Do you still think Mr. Watley is a good man?"

"Yes, I believe he is a very good man."

"Do you like him?"

"I suppose you could say that I like him." Jane felt her cheeks flush.

"Then you should speak to him, ask his forgiveness for dancing with other men when you were supposed to be making people believe you were engaged. Apologize for your part of the quarrel. Jane, if he's a good man, you should marry him."

"He doesn't want to marry me." Jane was surprised to feel a prickling behind her eyelids and a hollow feeling in her chest.

"How do you know?"

"He said so."

"He said he didn't want to marry you?"

"We both said it, more or less, although not in those exact words. I'm sorry, Catherine. I don't think I can decipher the books today. I suppose I'm tired from the trip."

"I don't doubt that. You've had a harrowing experience. Why don't you go home and take a nap."

"You look rather tired yourself." Jane noticed the

dark circles under her friend's eyes. "Is everything all right?"

"I haven't been sleeping very well. I've had some nightmares. But I am well enough."

Jane squeezed her friend's hand. "Why don't you let me stay the rest of the day while you go home and get some rest."

"Absolutely not. Now go home."

"I'll make it up to you," Jane said. "I'll stay late tomorrow and you can go home early."

"Molly is coming in to take my place tomorrow so I already have that arranged."

"Very well. I know better than to argue with you."

"Yes, you do. Now go home." Catherine playfully pushed Jane toward the door. "And don't come in tomorrow if you don't feel up to it. The books can wait."

It was raining rather hard, so Jane was grateful she had brought her umbrella. The guard offered to hire a hackney coach, but Jane refused. She didn't mind walking as long as she had her umbrella. But halfway home, the wind began to blow quite fiercely. She quickened her pace and was glad to finally make it. Her skirts were soaked from ankle to knee and her feet were quite frozen.

"Oh, Jane!" Penelope hurried toward her and helped her off with her wet jacket. "Fetch some hot water to Miss Gilchrist's room," she told the servant. "You are soaked to the bone." Penelope's forehead was creased in concern.

"I am well," Jane said, but her teeth betrayed her by chattering.

"I declare, this has been the coldest, wettest spring, and this is turning out to be quite a storm."

"I'm very glad Catherine lives above the shop so she doesn't have to go out in this." Jane would have sent the carriage for her otherwise.

Just then, Luke came into the hallway and his eyes locked on her.

Her stomach sank. Luke would see her looking like a drowned rat.

"Are you all right? You shouldn't be walking in this weather," Luke said, stating the obvious.

Penelope was hurrying her past him toward the stairs. "Henry is here," Penelope said, by way of explaining Luke's presence.

"I am well," Jane said, seeing that Luke was still staring at her. "Just a little wet." She smiled at the understatement.

When they reached her room, where the servants had brought a tub and were still bringing hot water, Jane groaned inwardly at Luke seeing her like that. But there was nothing she could do about it now.

"We must get you warm and dry before you catch your death." Penelope fussed over her as the maids set up a screen around the tub to give her the illusion of privacy.

"Don't worry, Penelope. I never get deathly ill."

As Jane soaked in the hot tub, she thought about what Catherine had said regarding Luke. Should she ask for Luke's forgiveness? After all, she couldn't really blame him for wanting to protect his son. Luke had wounded her pride but he hadn't actually done anything wrong.

She sighed. Life could be so humbling.

Chapter Twenty

Luke said a silent prayer that Jane would not get sick from walking in the cold wind and rain.

Henry's sister was a puzzle to him. She was strong-willed and spirited, independent and confident, but she was not like Anne, even though she had reminded him of Anne a few times. He saw now that she'd stirred up something inside him—pain, anguish over Anne and their relationship—but she was not to blame.

Perhaps he simply wasn't ready to marry. If time healed all wounds, he had not had enough of it yet, obviously.

"Luke? Did you hear me?" Henry interrupted his thoughts.

"Forgive me. My mind was wandering."

"I asked if you had had time to search your townhouse."

"I searched a bit. But Lenoir's men have also searched it, as you know. I even learned this morning that they had ransacked Camille's—Anne's friend's—home."

"Camille Dupre?"

"Yes. Do you know her?"

"I am acquainted with her. Is she not an associate of Lenoir's?"

"I believe she used to be his paramour, but she had fallen out of favor with him. Apparently she was so frightened that she has left England as of this morning. My servant told me of it."

"The servant who had been Anne's confidante?"

"Yes. But now that Camille has flown, what do you think of me sending that servant away? I do not trust the woman."

Henry seemed to consider the matter a moment, then said, "Yes, if you do not trust her, send her away. But first . . . have you asked her where Anne may have hidden that important paper?"

"I asked her. But I'm not sure she would tell me even if she knew."

"Then send her away. She is of no use to us, and we can follow her and see where she goes, where she finds employment next."

Luke nodded. "And I will search the house again—and try to think where else Anne may have hidden the paper."

"If it indeed exists," Henry said with a grim expression. "The man could have lied simply to keep his fingers and toes."

"I could pay him another visit, accuse him of lying and say we would take those fingers after all. That might jog his memory."

"I like your enthusiasm in pursuit of the truth. But perhaps we should use that as a last resort."

Luke realized he and Henry were both smiling. He also realized that, although he might still be feeling the pain and shock of what had happened with Anne and her nefarious activities, he was actually, in some way relieved. He felt a bit guilty to admit it, even to himself, but he'd been so distraught when she was alive, trying to figure out what to do, how to change her behavior, that now that she was gone . . .

Was he some kind of monster to feel relieved?

"Luke? Are you all right?" Henry's eyes showed concern rather than judgment.

"I am well. I think I'll go home and start searching again, if you have nothing further to discuss."

"Yes, go and search. Make sure the guards I sent are doing what they need to do to keep your household safe. How is your butler, by the way? Has he awakened?"

"He has been in and out of consciousness for the past two days, but even when he is awake, we can get no information from him that makes any sense. Either he doesn't remember what happened that day or his brain was so addled by the fall that he cannot talk about it."

"I will come by and see him when I have a chance, but keep me informed in the meantime. Also, Penelope wished me to invite you to dinner tomorrow night. Can you come?"

"Yes, please tell her I would be delighted to come for dinner tomorrow."

"And, Luke?"

"Yes?"

"I'm glad you are looking well lately, in spite of all that is happening. Something seems to be agreeing with you."

Luke suspected he was referring to how hollow-eyed and depressed he'd been after Anne's death. Luke certainly felt better now than he had in those first few months. And despite his misgivings about pretending to be engaged to Jane, he actually wondered if that—and Jane herself—had something to do with his improved mood.

Even though he wasn't sure what to do about her. One minute he was sure he'd never marry her if she were the last woman in London, and the next he was kissing her.

"Thank you. You have been a very good friend to me."

"You are a good man, Luke."

Why did his compliment touch something deep inside Luke's heart? Perhaps it was from growing up without a father, with very little family. But Henry's approval felt like the approval of a family member.

Luke nodded and hurried away before he embarrassed himself.

~ ~ ~

Jane felt a bit more like adding and subtracting numbers the next day as she made her way to the shop, this time taking the carriage since the rain was still coming down in sheets.

She'd been at her little desk barely an hour when Catherine poked her head in and whispered excitedly, "Luke Watley is here."

Jane's heart skipped a beat. He had already settled his late wife's accounts so he must be there to see her.

She stood, then sat down again. Should she go out to meet him? Or wait for him to come to her? She was still deciding what to do when he appeared in the doorway Catherine had just vacated.

Jane sprang to her feet.

"Forgive me for disturbing you at your work," Luke said, his hat in his hand, "but I wanted to ask how your throat is feeling and to make sure you were well after getting drenched yesterday."

"My throat is already much better, and I am quite well. Thank you for asking." Jane could feel herself smiling at the thought of his concern for her.

She might also be blushing, thinking of their kiss.

"I am glad to hear it. I was worried, since it was quite cold yesterday."

"I seem to be unscathed. I am blessed with a strong constitution, thankfully."

"Very good." He fidgeted with his hat, running his hands along the brim as he gradually turned it around. Then, as if he suddenly realized what he was doing, he stopped and let his hand drop to his side. "That is good to know."

"And are you well? Henry told me you were searching for a list." She said the latter words in a discreet whisper. "Is that going well?"

"All is well, though I have not found the item in question. I still hope to find it."

"That is good. Please let me know if there is anything I can do to help."

"Thank you. I cannot think of anything, unless you know of hiding places frequently used by young ladies."

"Have you looked under her bed? Of course you have. That is an obvious one."

"I have." He gave her his gentle smile.

How good he looked. He had such thick brown hair, and such kissable lips. Her heart turned over at remembering how it felt to kiss them.

What embarrassing thoughts she was prone to having these days!

Think, Jane. You were supposed to suggest hiding places.

"A good hiding place could be in the back of a

closet, perhaps a hidden pocket of some sort, attached to the back wall. I read about something like that in a novel once."

Luke nodded. "Ah, that is a good idea. I shall look."

"Indeed, it could be hidden anywhere in the house. Her room might be too obvious." Was she being too forward by mentioning Anne, even though she hadn't said her name?

"Yes, that is what I have concluded as well." Luke stared at the floor a moment, as if lost in thought.

"Or even outside the house. I once hid a letter I didn't wish my mother to see under the seat in the carriage."

Luke's expression suddenly changed. Did he suspect her of something illicit?

"It was my friend's letter. She was confessing a secret engagement of which her parents did not approve."

"Oh." Luke looked relieved.

"I promise, I have no secret engagements or other nefarious behaviors to confess," she said with what she hoped was a flirtatious look, as she smiled up at him through her eyelashes. "Only a pretend engagement," she added softly. *And a secret kiss.*

Luke cleared his throat, but he was smiling, thankfully. "I am glad to hear that."

She imagined herself stepping forward and kissing him again.

No, no, she couldn't. She mustn't. What would he think of her? But she wanted to kiss him again, and the very thought made her catch her breath.

Luke went on, obviously unaware of her temptation to kiss him.

"I wanted to say that I am very grateful that you

rescued Jeffrey from being kidnapped." He was fidgeting with his hat again. "I don't know if I even thanked you, but you have my utmost gratitude. Jane."

He said her name after a slight hesitation, his voice lowering in both octave and volume. It sent a pleasant sensation through her middle.

What would it be like to hear Luke say her name like that every day? She shivered, the same pleasant sensation moving through her.

"Are you cold?" He took a step toward her.

"No, I am well." She gazed up at him.

She had no excuse to kiss him. Before, she'd had the excuse of having just been through something frightening, of needing a warm embrace.

Perhaps she should have told him she was cold.

Jane pressed a hand over her mouth, stifling a laugh at her own ridiculous thoughts.

"Well, then, I suppose I shall see you tonight at dinner."

"Oh yes, that is good." She smiled brightly. "I shall look forward to seeing you tonight."

He smiled and took his leave.

She stepped out of her office to watch him walk across the shop. Just as he reached the door, he turned and looked back at her. He waved, a flick of his hand, put his hat on and was gone.

Catherine was watching her with a wide smile. "Fortunate girl."

Thankfully it was a slow day due to the rain and there were no customers in the shop.

"Whatever do you mean?" Jane ran her hands down her skirt, smoothing invisible wrinkles.

"You know what I mean. That man is in love with

you."

"You don't know that." Jane's stomach twisted as she realized she desperately wanted it to be true.

"I know he came to see you. Why would he come here? No one was here, so he's not trying to keep up the appearance that you are engaged. And he was obviously a bit nervous. Men don't get nervous when they visit a young lady who means nothing to them." Catherine crossed her arms, looking like she was waiting for Jane to confess.

Jane shrugged. "I don't think he was particularly nervous."

"But how do you feel about him? Do you still think of him as you used to, as the man every woman was in love with for no good reason other than that he was a young widower and they felt sorry for him?"

"I don't think I ever said that."

"Of course you did. Several times."

Jane took in a deep breath and let it out. "He is a good man who loves his son. Beyond that, I suppose one could also say he is brave and courageous when faced with danger. And he is earnest and eager to do the right thing." She could feel her cheeks flushing.

"You love him, don't you?" Catherine whispered.

Jane sighed again. "I think I do." She winced and chewed her lip.

"Then you must do something about it."

"And what is this thing I should do about it?" Jane folded her arms, mimicking Catherine.

Her friend suddenly threw her arms out wide. "I don't know but you must make him understand your feelings, for I am sure he already returns them."

"Would you have me be like those girls I saw at that

ball a few weeks ago who were flirting so much with him that he had to leave early to get away from them? I have never been one to shamelessly throw myself at a man."

"This is different and you know it. You have spent enough time together to understand his character, and he yours. There is no reason not to pursue his good opinion and to reveal your good opinion of him. Besides, I believe he already is in love with you, or at least well on his way to being in love."

Jane wondered if Catherine was right. She'd never felt this way before. Should she let Luke know of her feelings—feelings that were so new, she was still unsure of them?

Flirting and letting a gentleman know of her feelings of attachment for him had always seemed to go against both Jane's sense and her sensibility. But perhaps it was only her pride that held her back.

She suddenly had a niggling thought that perhaps those young ladies might be the wise ones, for instead of worrying what other people thought of them and trying to hide their feelings, they were making themselves available for love and marriage. They were going after what they wanted and believed would make them happy. After all, the gossips would not have any bearing on their future happiness. Why should they care what the gossips whispered about them?

Jane cared, even though she'd always said she didn't. But now she was thinking it was high time she stopped caring.

She groaned and put her head in her hands.

Chapter Twenty-One

When Jane arrived home, Penelope was coming down the stairs.

"There you are. I am sorry to say that instead of having a nice quiet dinner with only us and Luke, my late husband's cousin, Lord Hampstead, will be joining us for dinner. He's also bringing his wife and his wife's younger sister, Miss Campbell."

Penelope looked distracted as she glanced over her shoulder, back toward the kitchen.

"I'm sure all will be well," Jane assured her. "Luke knows how to make conversation, and Lord Hampstead is not too much of an ogre that we can't deal with him for one night."

"An ogre? No, not at all. But . . ." Penelope sighed. "Truth be told, he brings up bad memories for me." So seldom did Penelope frown or look distressed, but she was doing so now. "But that is not very gracious of me."

"It is all right to feel that way," Jane said, gently squeezing her shoulder. "But we shall get through it together. And from now on, even if he insists on inviting himself to dinner, just say no."

"He didn't insist. I just felt it was my duty to invite him, when he left his calling card, since I have yet to meet his new wife." But Penelope sounded tired, her eyes flitting away from Jane.

"You don't owe that man anything." Jane felt her temperature rising just thinking of all Penelope had suffered because of her first marriage. "Everyone knows your first husband's cousin is an insufferable, unremarkable man who is so full of himself he can barely see past the end of his nose."

Penelope's eyes went wide and she covered her mouth, but a small giggle escaped nevertheless.

Before she could berate herself for laughing at Jane's rude assessment of the Earl of Hampstead, Jane started toward the stairs. "I must go up and get ready for dinner. But don't worry. The dinner will go well, as we do not care for Lord Hampstead's good opinion, nor his new wife's, I daresay."

She hurried the rest of the way up the stairs, her heart lifting at Penelope's quiet laugh that she was no doubt trying to suppress.

Jane dressed carefully, thinking of Luke as she put on her favorite gown and instructed her lady's maid how to prepare her hair. Ready early, she went downstairs to wait for their guests.

She didn't have to wait long before hearing a voice in the entrance hall that made her heart flutter. Moments later, Luke was entering the sitting room where Jane was alone, reading a book.

He was early.

"Would you like something to drink? Some port, perhaps?" Jane smiled—her brother had once told her that men were put off by ladies who never smiled—and gazed into Luke's clear blue eyes.

~ ~ ~

Just as he'd hoped, Luke found Jane alone. But she looked so lovely, her smile so encouraging, it somehow made him even more nervous.

"I don't need a drink, I thank you. I came early, hoping to see you." *Hoping to spend time alone with you. Hoping to kiss you.*

"Oh?"

"Yes, I was wondering . . . I don't want to interfere with your work duties at the shop, but I was wondering if you'd—you may say no, of course, if you don't wish to." After looking down at his feet, Luke forced himself to look her in the eye. "Would you come to my home tomorrow morning and help me search for the list?"

"Of course." Jane's smile grew more animated. "I would like to help you search."

"You would?" He was half surprised she wasn't offended by his request. Many ladies would have been.

"Yes. It's like a novel, searching for a secret list, a list on which the lives of many people—and the fate of England—hangs in the balance." She clasped her hands together as if it was an entertaining outing to the lake country.

"Thank you. It is very important that we find this list." But instead of being desperate to find the list, his true motive for asking for her help was spending time with her.

"And we are still engaged." Jane raised her delicate eyebrows.

Was she trying to flirt with him? Or was she only teasing him? He remembered how she'd kissed him. They'd both behaved, ever since, as if it had never happened, but that kiss was never far from his thoughts.

One minute he reproached himself for letting

her get so deeply embedded in his thoughts, especially after Jane kissed him—something Anne had also done before they were married. And the next minute he was wondering how he might be able to spend more time with her. For the truth was, Jane was different, much more interesting than other young ladies. And when he was talking with her, all the ugly memories and emotions of the last couple of years faded away.

There were only two things left to determine. First, did Jane genuinely like him, or did she only want to get married? And second, was Jane as unfaithful as Anne?

Jane did not seem to be the kind of girl to try to manipulate a gentleman into asking her to marry him by kissing him. It *was* the kind of thing Anne would have done. Luke's fear was too strong; he had to be certain.

And the only way to be certain was to spend more time with Jane. And since he had tonight and the next day to do just that, he felt himself relaxing, more than he had in a very long time.

~ ~ ~

Jane's spirits lifted when Luke asked her to help him search his home for the list. He couldn't possibly need her help. Henry would give him all the men he needed, and Jane wasn't especially skilled in finding hidden things. So his motive must be to spend time with her. Her insides warmed just thinking about it.

Before she and Luke had time to say much else to each other, Lord Hampstead arrived with his new, very young wife and another young lady.

The new Lady Hampstead looked too young to even be out in Society yet. She must surely be older than she appeared. Lord Hampstead was thirty-five, so if she were only fifteen . . .

The poor girl.

Luke and Lord Hampstead began to converse, and Jane turned to Lady Hampstead and her sister, Gretchen. "How long have you been in London?"

"We arrived yesterday," Lady Hampstead said. "Lord Hampstead wished us to visit all his relations."

"Yes, you are newly married. Please accept my warmest wishes for your felicity."

"I thank you, Miss Gilchrist." She smiled—more of a smirk—and rearranged and smoothed her skirts. "We met at my coming out party a few months ago. Hamps was rather taken with me and proposed marriage the very next day."

She cut her eyes toward "Hamps" and he turned his head to glance her way, smirking back at his little bride, who was less than half his size.

Lowering her voice, Lady Hampstead said, "I can hardly believe I am married to an earl. I am a countess, and married before my older sister."

Gretchen stared back at Jane and mumbled, "And she never lets anyone forget it."

"You have nothing to complain of," Lady Hampstead said cheerfully. "Now that your brother-in-law is an earl, you shall have your pick of wealthy suitors."

Jane managed to force herself not to roll her gaze to the ceiling.

"Are you in need of suitors, Miss Gilchrist? If so, I can find you some, I am sure, now that I'm a married woman and there would be no competition between us." She smiled and her lips seemed to disappear.

"Indeed," Jane said.

There was a lull in the gentlemen's conversation, and Jane suddenly realized Luke was staring pointedly at her.

"My dear," Lord Hampstead said, "Miss Gilchrist is engaged to wed Mr. Watley."

Jane had momentarily forgotten about their charade.

"Mr. Watley?" Lady Hampstead asked. "How wonderful! Is he very wealthy?"

"This is Mr. Watley," Lord Hampstead said. "Mr. Luke Watley, here."

"Oh dear, I did not catch his name when we were introduced. It is a bad habit of mine, not paying attention to names, especially now that I'm married and have no need of . . . But let me congratulate you, Miss Gilchrist."

It was bad form to congratulate a lady on her engagement, as if she had won a prize, but Jane was amused rather than offended.

"He is rather wealthy," Jane said, smiling at Luke.

Luke smiled back at her. "I am the one to be congratulated, as Miss Gilchrist is the loveliest of ladies, both in appearance and character."

Jane wondered where Luke had read such a pretty sentiment. Perhaps she'd ask him later.

"Well done." Lady Hampstead clapped her hands, the sound muffled by her gloves. "I declare, these gentlemen could write poetry. What do you think, Miss Gilchrist? It is no wonder our heads are turned by the pretty speeches they make. I have told Gretchen time and again that under no circumstances should she marry a man who cannot give her every compliment. A woman wishes to be admired."

The girl was too young to be judged too harshly, but Jane did hope she found a wise matron to take her under her wing. Otherwise, she and her husband would attract only the kind of superficial friends that preyed on the foolish.

Luke and Lord Hampstead began to talk of hunting, and Lady Hampstead said, "Now that you are practically married, Miss Gilchrist, who among your acquaintances do you think my sister should set her sights on marrying? She prefers tall men who dress well."

"Carol, please stop."

"It is all right, Gretchen. Miss Gilchrist doesn't mind. We married women must stick together and help each other."

"I will be happy to introduce you to my acquaintances at the next opportunity," Jane said.

Penelope rushed into the room just then and welcomed her guests. "Forgive me for not being available when you arrived."

Jane wanted to reassure her that it was all right, since they were quite early.

Lady Hampstead went on with her embarrassingly gauche statements, smirking every so often at her husband, who usually gazed back at her with a confused look on his face, if he looked at her all.

Jane was glad when it was time to go in to dinner, and that she had been paired with Luke.

During dinner Henry joined them, and he and Penelope engaged their guests enough that Jane and Luke were occasionally able to converse while no one else was listening.

"I hope you didn't mind my visiting you at the shop yesterday," he said quietly. "I don't want to disturb you when you are working."

"I don't mind at all. I was not disturbed."

"I was concerned after I saw you had been out in

the rain the day before."

"Yes, you saw me in quite a state. I looked a fright."

"I did not see a fright. I saw a young woman who had been caught in the cold rain and might suffer ill effects from it."

"I suffered no ill effects."

"I am very glad."

He looked so warmly at her that her heart started to race and her gaze was inadvertently drawn to his lips, thoughts of their kiss once again at the front of her mind.

"Are you always so kind?" She felt slightly bewildered, an unfamiliar feeling.

"Not always. But I do try to be, whenever possible. I have my share of negative thoughts and feelings, I daresay. But I wish to be kind to those who are kind to me —to my fiancée, for example."

He smiled and she smiled back. But it did not feel as if they were playing a part. At this moment, it felt as if they truly were engaged.

"When I compare how you have been the last few days," she said softly, slowly, knowing she was treading on ground that would crumble if she was not careful, "with how things were in Hertfordshire . . ."

"I was not very kind then, was I? I said some things that were contentious, but I never imagined then that you—"

"What are you speaking of over there?" Lady Hampstead said quite loudly. "We ladies are making our way to the drawing room now and leaving the men to their port and cigars."

Everyone was standing up, so Jane and Luke stood as well. But her stomach was twisting. He never imagined that she what? What was he about to say?

She held Luke's gaze a moment. He was giving her quite an intense look. Would he finish what he was saying when they were together again? Surely not tonight. She sighed and followed the other ladies into the drawing room.

~ ~ ~

Luke's heart seemed to burn inside him while Jane played at the piano and he was able to watch her without guarding his expression, as the others were also watching and listening to her play. She often said she was not an accomplished player, but he probably would not have known if she made mistakes, and he thought she played beautifully. He was certainly glad to have an unobstructed view of her face. How serious she looked while she concentrated, an expression he didn't often see on her face, but she was no less beautiful.

He could no longer deny that he was falling in love with Jane Gilchrist.

For the longest time, he'd refused to believe that marrying Anne was a mistake. But when she'd practically admitted she was unfaithful to him, when "well-meaning" souls were telling him of her unscrupulous behavior while she was in London, the unsavory element with whom she was spending her time, he was forced to admit that he'd made a mistake. It had torn his heart in two. He'd actually carried a physical pain around in his chest for months, a pain that was made worse when he heard of her violent death.

He'd rather face a dozen giants in battle armor than make that mistake again.

When it was time to go home, Lord Hampstead and his talkative wife kept lingering, talking on and on. Finally, Luke felt so torn between staying and trying to say good-bye to Jane privately and his nervousness over what to say to her that he left abruptly.

Jane was probably used to his abrupt departures by now.

Chapter Twenty-Two

Jane sent word to Catherine that she would not be coming into the shop and went instead to Luke Watley's townhouse.

When she reached his door, she found her breathing was actually a bit shallow. She stopped and forced herself to take a deep breath and let it out slowly before knocking on the door.

Luke greeted her with, "I thought we would start looking downstairs, in the sitting room, unless you have an idea of somewhere else you would like to look."

"I was thinking we might look inside your clock. Do you happen to have a large clock?"

"There is one in the drawing room."

As he led her in that direction, she said, "I only ask because it was in the longcase clock that Penelope and Henry found something that had been hidden away by Penelope's first husband."

"Ah, I remember hearing of that."

"It is unlikely the list will be there, but . . ."

"It doesn't hurt to look, and it is a good idea for a hiding place." Luke turned into the drawing room and went to the longcase clock that stood against the wall and was almost as tall as he was.

He opened the glass case in front and looked around inside.

"While you do that, do you mind if I look around?"

"Please feel free to look anywhere."

"I feel as though I am snooping," Jane said, opening up a little door in a mahogany sideboard.

"Please don't worry. I am not hiding anything, and there is nothing you will see that I would be embarrassed about."

He said the words while his head was halfway inside the clock. He stood up and grabbed a candlestick, holding the light where he might see better inside the clock's dark inner workings.

Jane was glad to hear he wasn't hiding anything. She looked inside the sideboard, even feeling around at the back of it, searching for anything that felt like a piece of paper or even a crack where someone might hide a written list.

From the sideboard she moved on to the next piece of furniture, a small table which contained a drawer. Jane examined it but found only odds and ends: a candle nub, a quill pen, and a loose knob that looked to have fallen off another piece of furniture.

Luke stood and closed the clock case. "Nothing there."

They continued searching through the drawing room, looking behind paintings on the wall and testing the floor for loose boards.

"I think we can safely say it is not in the drawing room." Luke was staring at her. "Hold still. You have a spiderweb on your forehead." He gently brushed her forehead with his fingers.

"Oh. Thank you. I hope my hair is not a mess." She

felt for her hairpins, hoping they were not falling out.

"You look perfect." Luke was still staring at her.

"Shall we look in the sitting room now?" Jane turned away, her heart starting to beat fast.

Luke led the way and they did the same search they had executed in the drawing room.

As they worked their way around, Jane grew brave, as they were both focused on their tasks at opposite ends of the room. "Our conversation last night at dinner was interrupted. Do you remember what you were saying?"

He was down on his knees, looking underneath a small side table.

"I believe I was apologizing for what I'd said when we were in Hertfordshire." He stopped what he was doing and looked over his shoulder at her, giving her a lopsided smile. "I was convinced then that you did not care for me a whit."

"Why would you think that?" Jane's heart rose into her throat. She hoped he wouldn't answer that question.

"Well, I had proposed marriage to you and you refused me, preferring to *pretend* we were engaged, with the understanding that we would break it off in a few months."

"I didn't want you to feel obligated to me." Her face and neck were growing hot.

He seemed to be waiting for her to continue, alternately staring down at the floor and up at her.

"We didn't know each other very well," she explained, "and I want to marry someone who loves me."

He narrowed his eyes ever so slightly.

"You cannot find fault with me for that, can you?"

"No."

Her heart seemed to have stopped as she waited for

him to say something more.

Finally, he said, "We have been searching for a long time and you must be tired. Would you like to take a drive with me?"

"I have been enjoying the search, but a drive sounds very pleasant."

As they went to collect their gloves and hats and jackets, she noticed how attentive he was, how gentle while he helped her with her pelisse and waited for her to tie her bonnet's ribbon under her chin. When she compared him to how Lord Hampstead had treated his wife and her sister the night before, she realized that Luke was nothing like him. But he was a lot like her brother Henry.

Just as he was about to open the door for her, Jane stopped him.

"How many carriages do you keep here in London?"

"There are two carriages in the mews, the coach and a landau."

"Which one did Anne use most often?"

"The landau. It was her favorite." He frowned slightly.

"Let us take the landau. We can see if there are any hiding places inside it—unless you had rather not." She suddenly realized he probably had bad memories regarding Anne's favorite carriage.

"I think it is a good idea. In fact, I should have thought of it sooner. The landau hasn't been driven since —since she died."

Luke ordered the landau brought round to the front of the house and they soon were inside with the top down, as the weather was finally improved—cold, but no longer raining.

"Just to let you know," Luke said, speaking first, "I have brought along a pistol." He reached inside his coat and showed her the silver handle of a gun. "Under the circumstances, I decided to carry one with me when I leave home."

"That is probably a good idea," Jane said, "under the circumstances."

As the carriage was moving along at a jaunty pace, Jane happened to glance toward the sidewalk. "Lenoir! That looks like Lenoir!"

She pointed frantically and Luke strained to look.

"He's standing right there on the street."

"I believe it was Lenoir." Luke moved to sit down on the cushion next to Jane.

"He was looking straight at us." Jane's shoulders suddenly felt tense, exactly how she'd felt after the kidnapping and the attempted kidnapping in Hertfordshire.

Luke instructed the driver to head toward the Gilchrist townhouse so he could inform Henry of Lenoir's whereabouts. Then he sat back down beside Jane.

"Don't worry. All is well. We're past him now, and I am prepared for anything he might try." His hand went up to rest on his coat where the gun was hidden.

Luke was sitting so close his arm was pressed against hers. But she didn't mind. Part of her wished he would put his arm around her. But if they ever wanted this to be over, they had to find that list.

"Let's look under the seats." Jane stood in the jostling carriage and lifted the seat cushion where Luke had just been sitting. She drew out a blanket. Underneath that was a warming pan, but there was nothing else.

Luke helped her put the things back and replace the

cushion, then they turned and lifted their seat cushion. Inside was nothing except a piece of paper, folded like a letter, with the initials "L. W." written on the outside.

~ ~ ~

Luke snatched up the piece of paper with his initials on it, then let the seat fall back into place. He unfolded the paper and sat down.

His breath was stuck in his throat. He quickly scanned the words on the page, distinctly written in Anne's dramatic, sloping hand.

It was a list of names, many of them familiar names of Members of Parliament, business owners, and at least one constable. There was not one other thing on the paper. Only names.

His heart had lifted at finding the list, but it sank again when he saw there was no personal note. Had he truly hoped she would write some sort of explanation or apology?

"It's the list," he told Jane, then told the driver to go as speedily as possible to Henry Gilchrist's home.

He swallowed the lump in his throat and turned to Jane. "You did well. You found the list."

"*We* found the list. That is good. Perhaps now we won't be attacked in our homes or while leaving a ball." Jane gave him a crooked smile.

"Yes." He tucked the list inside his coat pocket, on the opposite side from his gun, then turned sideways on the seat to face her. "Jane, I would like to—" Suddenly Luke noticed a horse and rider following at almost a gallop, and gaining on them.

Jane turned to look and cried out. "That's one of Lenoir's guards."

"Faster!" Luke called to the driver.

The carriage jolted forward but not nearly fast enough to outrun the horse and rider. People on the edges of the street were glaring at them. But just as they turned onto Jane's street, he heard a shot ring out.

Over his shoulder Luke saw the rider was pointing a pistol at them. "Get down!"

Luke grabbed his pistol in one hand and pushed Jane's head and shoulders down onto the seat with his other hand.

"Get down on the floor," he said as another shot rang out.

He took aim and shot at the rider, hitting him in the shoulder.

The carriage careened to one side of the street, and Luke saw that the driver was slumped over and not moving.

One of their rear wheels hit a lamppost, and the carriage lurched sharply to that side. The wheel came off and the axle screeched as it struck the flagstones. It dragged along for several feet before stopping.

Only then did Luke realize he was holding Jane in his arms, bracing with his feet against the side of the carriage, his back propped against the seat.

Jane was gazing up at him, unblinking.

Luke was still clutching his gun in his hand behind Jane's back, pointed away from her.

"Are you all right?" he asked her.

She nodded. As they started to rise from the floor of the carriage, he heard the clatter of hooves coming toward them.

The man who shot the driver held a gun pointed at them. He and his horse were only ten feet away. He held his other arm tucked against his side, while a dark stain widened at his shoulder.

Luke pointed his gun at the man as he moved away from Jane, hoping to draw the man's aim away from her.

Another horse and rider suddenly trotted into view. It was Lenoir. He must have taken a shortcut through side alleys to get to Henry's house, only a hundred feet away.

A small crowd was starting to form, but at a distance, watching, gasping and wide-eyed.

"He will shoot you," Lenoir said in his French accent.

"And if he does, I will shoot him, and I will kill him." Luke's blood was boiling, heating his forehead and neck. But he had never been more serious, aiming his gun at the man's head, his sights pointing between his eyes. And at this close range, Luke would not miss.

"Give me the list," Lenoir said.

Luke said nothing. Then, out the corner of his eye, he saw Lenoir approaching with his own gun in his hand.

"Stay back," Luke said. "I will shoot him and then you. This is a repeating pistol and I still have enough shots to kill you both twice over."

Lenoir stopped. "Go ahead and shoot him, because we will both shoot you and then you can kill only one of us, but you'll be dead either way."

He was right and Luke knew it. But how displeased was the henchman that Lenoir cared so little for his survival? Luke couldn't tell, though he did notice a twitch in the man's jawline.

Either way, his only hope was that the henchman cared too much for his own life to shoot him.

~ ~ ~

Jane silently berated herself for not bringing her own pistol. Her brother had given her a smaller one in case she wished to carry it in her purse, but she had not brought it with her. In her state of heightened awareness of danger, she was certain she could aim it at Lenoir and at least incapacitate him. But even if she did, all four of them could end up dead, as close as they were to each other.

"Give me the list and I will let you both live," Lenoir said. "But if you don't, I will shoot you both."

"Very well. I will give it to you."

"Where is it?" Lenoir asked.

"It's in my coat pocket, right side."

Lenoir took a step toward him. The hateful man kept coming, even while Luke and the henchman kept their guns trained on each other. Finally, letting his gun drop to his side, Lenoir reached into Luke's pocket and drew out the paper.

With one hand he flipped it open, glanced at the names, then folded it and stuck it in his own pocket. "Thank you very much," Lenoir said, backing away.

A loud shot—so loud it was more like two shots at once—rang out. Jane screamed and stared hard at Luke.

Somehow Luke was still holding his gun, looking one way, then the other.

Lenoir was crying out and staring at his hand, the one that had just been holding a gun but was now empty and spurting blood. Meanwhile, his henchman was lying on the ground, not moving.

Then Jane saw Henry and half a dozen men approaching cautiously from the direction of the house, all with guns raised.

Luke turned and saw them too, finally lowering his

pistol and wrapping his arms around Jane.

She embraced him back, her heart beating so hard it hurt her chest.

"You're alive. Thank God. Thank God," she said, almost choking on the words.

She noticed her legs were trembling from bracing against the side of the carriage, which was resting at an angle on its broken axle.

"Are you injured?" Luke said, pulling away to look at her. His hands held onto her shoulders, and his hungry eyes took her in from her waist to the top of her head.

"No, I am well. And you?" She searched his face and upper body, making sure there was no dark red stain blooming anywhere.

"Yes, I think so."

Henry was beside the carriage, reaching up to help her down. But she pretended not to see him, instead clinging to Luke's arms.

Nothing seemed to matter at all anymore except that Luke was not hurt.

Chapter Twenty-Three

Jane held on to Luke's arm as they walked the rest of the way to her home.

Luke stayed and had tea with them after Henry left to tend to his two injured prisoners, Lenoir and his henchman. They discussed with Penelope what had happened, as well as the implications of the list of people —British citizens of good reputation—involved with Lenoir and his nefarious plans to infiltrate and eventually overthrow the government.

All Jane could think about was how close Luke had come to being killed. Her hand shook as she lifted her teacup and brought it to her lips, shook when she took a bite of a tart, shook when she touched her napkin to her lips.

And her eyes kept going to Luke, to where he sat in the chair between her and her sister-in-law, talking about Lenoir and the list.

She noticed his gaze moved to her almost as often as she looked at him.

Penelope was more talkative than usual, expressing her relief, shock, and fear by turns as she talked of what had happened. She seemed to understand that Jane was not herself, that she was still shocked.

Indeed, Jane found it difficult to speak without tears coming into her eyes, so hearing Penelope's voice was rather soothing.

Thank you, Penelope. You are such a good friend. She couldn't say the words out loud or she would start to cry, and she wanted them to think she was brave.

She took another sip of tea, trying to take comfort in its warmth, as the weather had suddenly become stormy again, the wind rattling the shutters as raindrops began to smack the windowpanes.

People started to call, braving the weather, expressing concern, having heard about or even seen what happened in the street. So many came that Penelope had to turn some away. But Jane just sat and sipped her tea, letting Penelope answer their questions while she checked to make sure Luke was still alive, still unharmed, and still sitting two feet away from her.

Henry came home in the middle of calling hours. After the callers had been there an appropriate amount of time, Henry asked them to leave to allow the family to rest after their ordeal.

Why was Jane so unnerved? She'd been kidnapped once, her room invaded in the middle of the night, and bruised and threatened a second time, but she'd never been so emotional as she was now.

I love him. That was it, she finally realized, and it was both the logical and the emotional explanation. She loved Luke Watley, and he'd nearly been killed right in front of her.

When Luke stood to go Jane followed him to the door, noticing that her brother and sister-in-law stayed in the sitting room. She was alone with Luke.

He embraced her, holding her close while he

pressed his face against her hair. "I thank God you are safe. Thank you, God." His voice was low and his breath warmed her ear.

He quickly let her go and stepped back. "Forgive me if I am overstepping." He let his voice trail off, then reached for the door. "I'll be back tonight," he said abruptly.

But she couldn't bear to let him go without saying something. She grabbed his hand before he could open the door. "I am so thankful you are safe, so glad you weren't hurt." She had to blink back tears and clung to his hand, willing him to kiss her.

If only he would.

"Thank you for that," Luke said. He squeezed her hand, then kissed it quickly and was out the door, leaving her to sigh in disappointment.

~ ~ ~

The workmen had been in Jane's room for an hour, installing the bars on her window.

"I don't need the bars now," she had told Henry. "Lenoir has been captured and we have all the names of those who were trying to help him start a revolution."

"Better to be safe than sorry," Henry replied.

Jane remained in the library with the door closed, lying on the couch and reading a book—or trying to read, rather. Her mind kept wandering to the events of earlier in the day, to Luke and to their adventures. She tried to remember every expression on his face, everything he had said. Was he as exhausted as she was after nearly being killed, after holding his gun on another man?

Jane sighed, wishing she could talk to him, ask him how he felt when Lenoir and his henchman were threatening them. She wanted to know all his thoughts.

Did he love her? She was like the person playing the silly game with the flower petals, picking them off and saying, "He loves me, he loves me not," as she went back and forth in her mind, trying to figure it out.

"The workmen are finished with your window." Henry was standing in the doorway of the library, and Penelope was beside him. But there was something strange about the way they were both smiling at her.

"What?" Jane asked, rising from the couch. "What have you done?"

"We haven't done anything," Penelope said, but her smile did not fade.

"Come and see your window," Henry said.

"Why should I? I've seen iron bars on a window before."

"Well, isn't it time for you to change for dinner?" Penelope asked. "You should go up to your room and change."

"You have done something," Jane said. "What is it?"

"Nothing, nothing at all," Penelope insisted, and she never lied. "Just come upstairs with me. Please?"

"All right." Jane put down her book and went with Penelope.

As they climbed the stairs, Penelope giggled.

"I can hardly wait to see what it is that has you so excited," Jane said. "But I have to say, it's a bit annoying that you're not telling me what it was."

Penelope's smile was not the least bit diminished by Jane's annoyance.

Jane entered her room. "There are no bars on my window. Why are you and Henry being so strange today?" Didn't they know she'd had enough shocks and surprises for one day?

Penelope stood by the door, grinning like a mischievous child.

"And what am I supposed to do now?"

"Go to the window," Penelope said, "and look out at the street."

Jane went to the window and looked down. There, covering the sidewalk and half the street, were mounds and mounds of yellow and blue flowers. And in the middle of them stood Luke Watley.

Jane gasped and leaned out the open window.

Luke was staring up at her. A crowd had gathered on the sidewalk across the street.

"Jane Gilchrist," Luke said in a loud voice.

"Yes?" She giggled in spite of herself.

"I love you passionately, wildly, madly, and I can't live without you. Will you consent to be my wife and love me forever?"

Jane's heart seemed to seize in her heart, and she could hear the gasps from the women in the crowd all the way from the other side of the street.

"I will!" she called down to him, smiling and crying at the same time. "I love you too, Luke Watley!"

Jane covered the lower part of her face with her hand, knowing she was about to start crying in earnest. When she was able to control herself, she said, "Come inside."

Jane closed the window and ran out of her room, past Penelope, past Henry, and she was hurrying through the entrance hall when Luke came in the door and shut it behind him.

She threw her arms around him and kissed him, but briefly, since she was sure Henry and Penelope were watching, not to mention a few servants who were probably peeking out of various rooms and the staircase, which was in plain view.

"I love you," Jane whispered against his cravat.

"I'm so sorry for the hurtful things I said to you," he whispered back, his lips next to her ear. "I don't want to imagine my life, or Jeffrey's, without you."

"Are you sure you love me?" Jane went on in a whisper. "I can be stubborn and willful, and I do things that I know Society doesn't approve of. But I promise I will love you and Jeffrey with all my heart."

He was holding her close, squeezing her, even, between his arms. "I told you. I love you passionately, wildly, madly, and I want everyone to know it. No more pretense, no more fake engagements. I want you in my home as my wife as soon as I can procure a license."

Jane's heart beat faster at his impassioned words. There were so many things she could say, many intimate, vulnerable things that she couldn't say. Finally, what came out of her mouth was, "Thank you for the flowers, but I don't think they will all fit in the house."

He gave her a playful squeeze.

"It was a beautiful, wonderful, grand gesture." She lifted her head and looked up into his face. "Thank you."

"Let us be the first to wish you every happiness," Henry said somewhere behind her.

Jane reluctantly released her hold on Luke and turned to face her brother and sister-in-law.

"Jane is wondering what we shall do with all the flowers," Luke said.

Penelope was wiping a tear from her eye. "Oh my. I don't know."

"Perhaps we could give some away," Jane said.

The next thing she knew, she and Luke were

stepping out of the front door, and the crowd, which was still standing outside, began to clap their hands and cheer. Then the four of them spent the next half hour giving flowers away to the people. And even after they'd given away as much as people would accept, it took the servants ten minutes or more to bring the rest into the house.

When they were in the sitting room surrounded by flowers, they talked of plans and hopes for the future. They discussed the things they had said that they no longer meant. And they kissed, often, as Henry and Penelope had blessedly left them alone.

"I must go back to Hertfordshire in the morning," he said, "to speak to my bishop about a common marriage license and enter the bond."

He was serious about them being married right away, as the common license issued by the bishop of his parish would spare them from having to wait for the banns to be read. With a common license, they could be married immediately.

"May I go with you?" Would he think her terribly forward?

"I was hoping you would wish to come. We can stay and get married the next day at the parish church, if the clergyman is available."

Luke spent the rest of the day with Jane, staying for dinner that night. And just as dinner was over, the housekeeper announced, "A servant has come from Mr. Watley's house saying that Mr. Cobb, the butler, is awake and talking."

Luke said a quick good-bye and he and Henry left.

When Henry arrived an hour later, he said that Cobb had already identified Stokes, the man who was captured at Luke's country estate, as his attacker.

"And he shall recover?" Jane asked.

"He will be weak at first, but he should make a full recovery."

"That is wonderful." Jane clasped her hands together, wondering what else she could possibly wish for.

"You should be in bed," Henry said in his older brother voice. "You have a busy day tomorrow, traveling to Hertfordshire and preparing for your wedding."

"You are coming too, I hope."

"Penelope and I will be along for your wedding day after tomorrow."

"Well, enjoy this moment of telling me to go to bed, because I shall be married and you will not be able to command me as you have done, practically ever since I was born."

Henry only grinned. "I'm too pleased at the moment to argue with you."

~ ~ ~

Luke and Jane were married three days thence in a small ceremony in her parish church. And it was said that Jeffrey celebrated the most enthusiastically of all the guests, as every time they raised a glass to toast the newly wedded couple, Jeffrey squealed and clapped his hands.

In the evening Jane sang Jeffrey to sleep while Luke looked on. When they tiptoed from his room, leaving him asleep in his little bed, Luke took her by the hand and kissed her cheek.

"I am truly a fortunate man." He gazed into her eyes.

After all that he had been through, Jane was touched by his words. She ran her thumb over the stubble on his jawline. "I am the fortunate one."

Their lips met in a kiss that became more passionate, and Luke suddenly swept her up into his arms.

It was not Jane's nature to wish to be carried anywhere, but just this once, as he carried her the short way to their bedroom, she would enjoy letting her protective, good-hearted husband carry her wherever he wanted to go.

THE END

Stay in the Know!

Want to keep up with my new releases? Sign up for my newsletter here: Melanie Dickerson newsletter or on my website, https://melaniedickerson.com/

You can also follow me on Instagram @melaniedickerson123 or Facebook, MelanieDickersonBooks, to stay in the know, see the book covers before anyone else, and keep up with all my latest news.

If you click the Follow button on my Amazon profile page, https://www.amazon.com/Melanie-Dickerson/e/B003BAAJG6/ you will get an email whenever I have a new book releasing.

Thanks for reading my books and staying up to date. Feel free to message me on my social media or my website.

Please review my book! I am grateful for reviews or even just a rating on Amazon. Leaving a short review for a book you loved is so very helpful to the author! Thank you in advance!

IMPERILED YOUNG WIDOWS

A cruel faithless husband is murdered, his widow becomes the killers' next target. But a chivalrous hero is just around the next corner. Don't miss this exciting, romantic series set in Regency England!

A Perilous Plan

Penelope Hammond finds herself a widow at the age of twenty-three, having been married five years to a man she barely knew. Her husband, David Hammond, Lord Hampstead, was a member of the House of Lords who rarely said more than a few words to her in a week's time-- and often did not come home at night.

But Lord Hampstead was from a wealthy, powerful London family with no enemies, so why was he murdered?

Penelope is a penniless widow with few friends and only her cold grandmother to lean on. When she finds herself pursued by both English officials and French spies, she doesn't know who to trust—until a handsome Member of Parliament, Henry Gilchrist, saves her from being attacked and kidnapped. Mr. Gilchrist seems so determined to help her, but can she trust him?

When she starts to fall in love with the handsome young Member of the House of Commons, will he be too embittered from a former lost love to accept his own growing feelings? But first they must save themselves from those who would do them harm, or there will be no future for them, either together or apart.

A Treacherous Treasure

Rebecca Heywood thought marriage would make her happy, but that hope was destroyed by her husband's infidelity. When he is murdered, everyone assumes it was at the hands of the angry husband of one of his paramours. Then rumors emerge of a pirate's treasure buried somewhere on their estate, and she discovers a long-lost treasure map among her late husband's grandfather's papers. Could her husband have been murdered by treasure hunters?

Thomas Westbrook hoped for a quiet life in the country after the horrors of war. But when he hears a gunshot the day after his neighbor is murdered, he finds himself coming to the aid of the young widow. Falling for the widow of his back-stabbing former friend would be a grave mistake. But he feels drawn to the kind and beautiful Rebecca, and when her life is threatened, he realizes he would do anything to save her.

Rebecca can't imagine marrying again after her husband's many betrayals. She also can't deny her feelings for Thomas Westbrook. But how can she ever trust men, attraction, or marriage again—the very things that ruined her happiness?

Rebecca and Thomas must find the treasure first, before the murderers and would-be thieves, even as their growing feelings for each other wage war against all their deepest fears.

A Deadly Secret

Lillian Courtney's husband's criticizing and bullying ways culminate with him physically striking her, and she runs away to the Isle of Wight, taking her young daughter with her. Her husband follows her there—and is found dead the next day. Her mother-in-law accuses her of killing her husband, then tries to take her child away from her. Lillian is devastated at the prospect of losing her daughter.

Nash Golding, Earl of Barrentine, was not looking for trouble. He was only trying to keep his secret safe—the secret that he is a novelist publishing amusing satires under the pen name Perceval Hastings. His family would be aghast if his secret were made public. As an earl and a member of the House of Lords, working as an author of satirical novels is beneath him. But even more scandalous is his plan to marry the young widow, Lillian--a marriage of convenience, since he hardly knows her--to help ensure that she is able to keep her child.

Nash strives to keep the pretty widow safe from her late husband's devious family members, who wish to gain control of her daughter. But while he is protecting them, will his own secret be revealed? His position in society and in Parliament will be irreparably damaged.

Lillian is falling in love with the handsome earl, despite her fear and lack of trust. Nash, in turn, finds that neither his reputation nor his heart is safe when the lovely Lillian is near.

A Stormy Season

Nothing but the deepest love will induce Jane Gilchrist to marry, even when asked by the young and handsome widower with whom every other girl is in love.

Luke Watley lost his wife to a tragic accident. But when he discovers it was no accident at all, he must solve the mystery behind her murder, or he—and anyone close to him—is in danger of becoming their next victim.

Jane Gilchrist is maddeningly opinionated, annoyingly high-spirited, and . . . more appealing than any woman has a right to be. He seems to lose all rationality when she is near. But if he lets her get too close, she might be the next person to be killed because of his faithless first wife. But when her reputation is at stake, in an effort to do the right thing as a gentleman, he asks her to marry him. But when she agrees only to a pretend engagement, sparks of every kind begin to fly.

Jane is disgusted by the way women fawn all over the newly widowed Mr. Watley. She can't decide if she should hate him for being so sought after, feel sorry for him for losing his wife, or kiss him when no one is looking. Whatever she decides, it's sure to be a stormy season!

ACKNOWLEDGEMENT

This book was a lot of fun to write, but it would have been much more of a struggle if not for my writing accountability partner, Anne Marie Brehm, a.k.a. A. M. Costello! Thank you for writing with me the past several months. I'm very grateful for you and your friendship.

I need to thank my wonderful editor and friend, Natalie Nyquist, for her amazing work on this book. Thank you so much for all the suggestions, feedback, and line editing expertise!

I'm forever grateful for my brainstorming helpers, my daughters Faith and Grace, my husband Aaron, and Anne Marie. Thanks for letting me talk out my story with you and for offering suggestions and ideas. I love you guys.

I'm so happy I get to do this writing thing full time, and that is due to my amazing readers. Thank you so much for all your support!

DISCUSSION QUESTIONS

1. What are the reasons Jane Gilchrist originally wasn't interested in Luke Watley? Do you think some of her reasons were good, or were they somewhat irrational? Why or why not?

2. What are the reasons Luke wasn't interested in Jane? How did she remind him of his first wife, Anne?

3. Why did Luke conclude that Jane was not similar to Anne after all?

4. Why did Jane become a part owner in her friend Catherine's shop?

5. What qualities did Jane and Luke notice in each other when they were kidnapped and ultimately escaped?

6. Why did Luke ask Jane to marry him, initially? Why did she refuse him?

7. When Jane and Luke were pretending to be engaged, why did Luke ask Jane to keep her distance from Jeffrey? Do you think he was right to ask this?

8. At the ball at Luke's country house, why was Jane so offended when Luke went to talk with the men instead of dancing with her? What was the childhood memory that this triggered in her?

9. Have you ever overreacted to a situation because it triggered a painful or traumatic memory? Were you aware that you were being triggered in the moment, or did you only realize much later?

10. Do you think Luke was wise to say that he wanted to understand why he had been so attracted to Anne so that he wouldn't make the same mistake again? How could he go about figuring this out?

11. Jane thought, "Life could be so humbling." Do you agree? If so, how is this a good thing?

ABOUT THE AUTHOR

Melanie Dickerson

Melanie Dickerson Melanie Dickerson is the New York Times bestselling author of Regency Romantic Suspense and Medieval fairy tale retellings. Her novels have won the Christy Award, the National Reader's Choice Award, the Golden Quill, Book Buyer's Best Award, and more. Since she was a kid, Melanie has been writing stories involving a hero and heroine, lots of adventure, and a happily ever after ending. Now you'll find her in North Alabama watching movies with her handsome husband and her oddly calm (and just plain odd) Jack Russell terrier, writing with her accountability partners on video chat, or daydreaming about the characters and plot of her next book.

Printed in Great Britain
by Amazon

48839915R10148